Dear Reader,

Welcome to Wilinski's Fight Academy, Boston's shadiest boxing and mixed martial arts gym!

Don't know much about mixed martial arts? If not, join the club! Jenna, this story's heroine, doesn't even know what MMA stands for until she shows up to claim the property she's inherited from her late, estranged father.

And since you're holding a Harlequin Blaze book in your hands, I can only assume you also share Jenna's love of all things romantic. *Making Him Sweat* is the first in a series of stories set in the unlikely cross-section where Jenna's fledgling matchmaking business collides with the realm of her downstairs neighbors—a gritty basement full of battered boxers. It's all about opposites attracting, and Jenna just might meet her own match in the disreputable gym's general manager, Mercer. His love of fighting is as foreign to Jenna as her romantic idealism is to him, which made throwing these two into the ring together all the more fun!

I hope you enjoy it! And if you finish this story wanting more, keep an eye out for the next book in the series, when hot-blooded Rich goes head-to-head with Jenna's pretty new assistant.

Happy reading!

Meg Maguire

Making Him Sweat

—

Meg Maguire

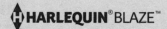

Recycling programs
for this product may
not exist in your area.

ISBN-13: 978-0-373-79744-8

MAKING HIM SWEAT

Copyright © 2013 by Meg Maguire

Printed in U.S.A.

ABOUT THE AUTHOR

Before becoming a writer, Meg Maguire worked as a record-store snob, a lousy barista, a decent designer and an overenthusiastic penguin handler. Now she loves writing sexy, character-driven stories about strong-willed men and women who keep each other on their toes...and bring one another to their knees. Meg lives north of Boston with her husband. When she's not trapped in her own head, she can be found in the kitchen, the coffee shop or jogging around the nearest duck-filled pond.

Books by Meg Maguire

HARLEQUIN BLAZE
608—CAUGHT ON CAMERA
734—THE WEDDING FLING

To get the inside scoop on Harlequin Blaze and its talented writers, be sure to check out blazeauthors.com.

Other titles by this author available in ebook format.
Don't miss any of our special offers. Write to us at the following address for information on our newest releases.

Harlequin Reader Service
U.S.: 3010 Walden Ave., P.O. Box 1325, Buffalo, NY 14269
Canadian: P.O. Box 609, Fort Erie, Ont. L2A 5X3

For Amy, Ruthie and Serena,
with crazy gratitude for your time and input.
You gals rock my socks. Continually.

Also with thanks to the staff of the Wai Kru
mixed martial arts gym in Allston, Massachusetts—
especially Michael, for letting me loiter and ogle,
and pester him with endless questions about
the business of building great fighters.

And of course, thank you to my editor, Brenda,
for liking this premise enough to
contract the series, and for beating my first draft
into submission. I won't let you down, coach.

1

Jenna's heels clicked against the asphalt as she crossed the street. Though they'd proven adorable enough to earn compliments from three different strangers on the ten-minute walk, she'd have to rethink this shoe choice in the future. Boston was made for flats, with its warped old brick sidewalks. Made for flats and for doctors who specialized in ankle injuries.

She survived a final block to reach her destination, a building she'd seen only in photos until this moment. Five stories, a former hosiery factory long since divided and repurposed. She paused to picture a new sign above the entryway, but a river of speed-walkers engulfed her, their brusqueness making it known that 9:00 a.m. downtown was not the time and place for daydreaming.

Leaving the August sunshine behind, she stepped into a cool, wide front corridor, with a worn but handsome hardwood floor and brick walls. She smiled, clutching her purse with cautious hope. With a bit of polishing and some nice light fixtures and greenery, this place could be very stylish indeed.

To her right stood a display case of boxing equipment, its glass overdue for some Windex. Gloves and shorts, headgear, mouth guards, supplement bottles—the accessories of her inheritance, surreal as that felt. She eagerly erased the image on her mental sketchpad and filled in the blanks, adding a couch and a couple of easy chairs, a shiny coffee table covered in magazines. Hopeful, excited people chatting as they waited. Waited for Jenna to make their romantic dreams come true.

In a few months' time, this would be the home of the Boston branch of Spark, New England's fastest growing matchmaking company—and Jenna its newest franchise owner. Spark was very old-school, unlike the online services, and that suited Jenna just fine. The web was great for impulsive commitments—such as shoes you'd never tried on—but one's love life was not a thing to march into blind. Finding Mr. or Miss Right could be mystifying, and as a future matchmaker she was excited to help shine some light through the fog.

At the end of the foyer was a wide stairway leading down to what a banner on the wall proclaimed Wilinski's Fight Academy—the less savory half of Jenna's real estate inheritance. At the sight, she dropped back to earth from the clouds. The front doors opened behind her, and she tensed as a stocky man toting a gym bag brushed past and disappeared down the far steps. The misgivings she'd been flirting with for the past couple months flared, setting her body buzzing.

To her left was an office fronted with tall windows, welcoming if not private. Beyond the glass a man sat at a desk, typing on a laptop. If this was who she thought it was, he'd be expecting her. But not the news she had to share.

She took a final, calming breath and approached the open door, studying her adversary before announcing her arrival.

The man looked about thirty, with short brown hair. His thick arms and the formidable build beneath his T-shirt told her he was no stranger to the gym's recreational punishment. His physique made her heart race. In another context it would've been a guilty, pleasurable excitement, but this thumping at her pulse points was pure nerves. A strong, capable body might be an asset for a lover—if you were into that kind of thing, which Jenna most certainly was *not*—but intimidating from an opponent. And this man was likely to prove himself the latter, once she spelled matters out for him.

She straightened the sweep of her bangs, the hem of her skirt, the set of her shoulders. Abandoning her silly, day-dreaming self at the threshold, she knocked on the doorframe.

The man looked up and she saw him scan her in a breath before rising. He had a stern, pensive expression, but she thought she caught a widening of his eyes.

"Jenna?"

She stepped inside. "Yes. Are you Mercer Rowley?"

"I am. Nice to finally meet you." He came around the desk to shake her hand in his rasped one, the gesture gruff and un-giving, just as she'd expected. No doubt his personality would prove identical.

Still, he was younger than she'd imagined. She'd assumed her father would have left some late middle-aged casualty of the sport at the helm, someone like himself. Well, someone like the character Jenna's mother and the internet had painted for her in broad, unflattering strokes.

Mercer wheeled an ancient office chair from the corner for Jenna, and took a seat on the edge of the desk. He studied her as she got settled.

"Yes?" she prompted.

"Wow. Jenna Wilinski. You've got your dad's eyes." He said it slowly, a softness overtaking his voice and face. His gaze moved all over her body. Not ogling, but assessing.

Two could play that game.

Her brain clicked into pro-mode, making an inventory the way the matchmaking seminar she'd completed the previous month had taught her to.

Mercer had a boxer's nose if she'd ever seen one, broken who-knew-how-many times, and homely ears to match. One scarred eyebrow not as tidily angled as the other. *Fearless.*

Deep, steady breaths—*calm under pressure.* Perhaps a comforting presence for an anxious woman, or a foil to a chaotic one. He'd chosen a competitive, physical vocation, appealing to a passionate, ambitious type, should he somehow end up in Jenna's singles database. Though as a selling point, "local color" probably should not equal black-and-blue.

"So," she said. "My father left you in charge."

Mercer nodded. "I've been training here since I was fifteen, under your dad. Then I started working with the younger guys about three years ago, and managing some aspects of the business. Your dad was grooming me for it the last year or so. Since his final hospitalization."

Her stomach soured at the realization this stranger had known her father infinitely better than she had. That they'd shared a sport, a working-class accent, some brutal male appetite. That he'd known her father was dying, when she hadn't been informed he'd had so much as a cold. The man from a handful of old photos, holding her as a baby, carrying her on his massive shoulders when she was a tiny kid. The man from old news headlines, convicted of drug-running and money laundering fifteen years earlier, out of this very building. The sentence had been overturned during an appeal, due to insufficient evidence, but as far as nearly everyone was concerned, Monty Wilinski had been guilty.

"Well, welcome to your inheritance," Mercer said. "Do you have any interest in fighting? In overseeing the gym, I mean."

"No, none at all."

His smile was mild, but warm. She suspected he could have been quite good-looking, if he'd chosen vanity over violence. *Striking* was how she'd package him to a potential date. A dangerous, inadvisable breed of sexy, the kind that didn't let a woman ever truly relax. His unwavering gaze made her feel all squirmy and…naked. She clutched her purse strap to still her hands.

"Yeah, your dad didn't expect you'd be interested," Mercer said. "Though it was nice of you to come all the way to Boston and see what you've signed up for. I'm happy to keep running the place. It shouldn't give you too much trouble."

Perhaps not, but this man might.... She decided to tear off the bandage, no point dancing around the issue. "It was a stipulation of my father's will that I keep the gym open."

He nodded.

"But only through December thirty-first." Her body went strange and cool and calm as the words rushed out.

Mercer's lips parted but he didn't speak for several seconds. "Okay. Right...so. And then what happens? You're not thinking of closing it, are you?"

"I don't know." She hated how hard and stuffy she sounded, but this was her first act as a businesswoman and a boss, and she was determined to prove herself an assertive one. Or fake it. "It's quite likely that I might."

Mercer sat up straight, brows drawn into a tight line. "Why would you do that?"

"It hasn't turned a profit in eighteen months."

He slumped. "Well, no. But we're not hemorrhaging money, either. It's just been a rough patch, with your dad being sick, and the economy... It'll bounce back. Keep it open and you won't have to think twice about it, aside from getting deposits in your account back in California or signing the random piece of paper—"

"I've moved to Boston, actually. As of this morning."

He blinked, hazel eyes going glassy as he processed the news. "What do you think you'll do if you shut us down? Sell the property? The market's not great—"

"I'm not selling it. If I do decide to close the gym, I'll probably rent the basement to an outside business." She indicated the office they were in. "I'm going to use this floor for a company I plan to open."

"You're going to close an established business to gamble on a new one?"

Jenna steeled herself, an invisible bell clanging to announce the official start of their bout. Her blood warmed and fizzed with adrenaline. Let the debate begin.

"It's not a matter of choosing one business over another. But I've sunk all my savings into a franchise I'm investing in, and I'm not bankrupting myself to keep the gym on life support. The basement rental could bring in close to ten grand a month. Can the gym do that?"

His face fell. "It's never made that much."

She'd seen the past decade's bank statements—she knew it didn't. Even in good years, the profit it turned was a modest one. The gym was only still in business because her father had owned the space outright, and because he'd loved the place too much to put it out of its misery, even after the scandal had gutted its membership and scared away all its former sponsors. Without doubt, he'd loved it more than his family. Jenna and her mom could have used that money in the early days, back when they'd essentially been homeless, moving every six months, crashing with one set of relatives after another.

"Unless something seriously changes, the gym's a charity I can't afford to support."

"It's your inheritance."

"The property's my inheritance. My dad's will made that clear, and I'm happy to conform to his instructions and keep it open until the New Year. It's the least I can do, considering he left me a nice little slice of Downtown Crossing."

Mercer's eyes narrowed, wrecking his poker face. A humorless smirk quirked his lips. "Unless you want to load this building onto a truck and move it a block north, you're in Chinatown."

Fine, it wasn't Summer Street, but it had a downtown zip code, and was rent-free. Jenna didn't stand a chance of topping this windfall ever again in her life, short of winning the lottery.

Two men in sweat-streaked shirts sauntered past the office windows, glancing in and making Jenna feel distinctly as though she'd been locked in one of those submersible shark-observation cages.

"You can't close this place." If Mercer was panicking, he hid it well. Jenna's own heart was thumping hard. She dreaded confrontation, but Mercer looked like six feet of unflappable muscle wrapped in a white T-shirt. Why did that make her feel so damn edgy?

"It was your dad's whole life, this gym."

Yes, indeed it was. "As much as this place might mean to you, it's my choice. And I haven't made my decision yet. I'm not allowed to until the end of the year, and you're welcome to try to change my mind," she added as a consolation. Jenna thought that time would be far better spent looking for greener pastures. "But this place has been in the red the past year and a half. And it's got enough savings to stagger on for another, what? Maybe two years, at this rate, before that account's bled dry?"

Mercer's jaw clenched. "And I can tell you all the reasons why we're in the red, and all the things that can be done to change that."

"I'm sure you can." And she was sure there'd be some ugly debates in her future over whether she'd be financing any improvements Mercer might have in mind. The gym needed full-on head-to-toe plastic surgery, but its budget would barely cover a concealer stick. Any money she agreed to sink into these changes would surely be too little, far too late. He hadn't bothered suggesting she sell the gym itself. He knew as well as she did—as even the most foolish investor would—it was a lost cause.

He rubbed his face. "What do you want the ground floor for, anyhow? Why not rent that out?"

She felt her cheeks color, embarrassed to admit such a girlie endeavor to this no-nonsense man. "I'm opening a match-making business."

"Wait. Like fight promotions?"

"No. You know, *matchmaking.* Arranging dates between compatible people?"

Mercer's eyebrow rose, the one not hampered by scar tissue.

"Legitimate, romantic dates," she elaborated, in case he was imagining something more akin to an escort service.

"Hasn't that gone extinct? Don't all those desperate people just go online these days?"

"Not everyone. Some people don't want to shop for a relationship the way they might for car insurance or…" She trailed off, knowing her own feelings on the matter must be showing. "Anyhow, it'll cater to busy professionals, people who want a personalized, more traditional approach to dating. And it's not desperate at all. It's very practical."

"And you'll be using the office for that?"

"I will. So during the time the gym stays open, I'll need to move the display cases and everything in here downstairs."

Mercer's gaze swiveled to the ceiling, nearly an eye-roll. "Of course you will."

"Don't look so annoyed. I'm being put out, too, you know, consulting with potential clients with bruised, sweaty men staggering past the windows." She jerked her head toward the entryway, just as another such specimen went by.

"Some women might like that."

Jenna shot him a skeptical look.

"When's all this going down? Your evil plans and this new business?"

"My evil plans? I'm not the bad guy here. I know what this

place is about. I've read the articles." She eyed the desk, wondering if that was where her father had sat, funneling drug money through the gym's accounts.

"That was more than a decade ago. And it was a handful of assholes who did that, not your dad. He was acquitted."

Not before he was convicted, and just after a whole bunch of evidence was very conveniently mishandled.

Mercer leaned to the side, bracing a palm on the desk. It was unnerving, being in this room with this man, sitting feet apart in the same space, at complete and utter odds. There was tension crackling between them, hot and sharp, an electrical current. She wondered if this was what stepping into a boxing ring felt like, conflict as visceral as lust.

Round two, she thought. He'd come out slow, scouting for her weak spots, maybe; now he'd surely start swinging. But he surprised her, his tone turning soft and sincere.

"If your dad was guilty of anything all those years ago, it was trusting the wrong people. He put his faith in guys like me, but that time he got burned. Bad."

"Maybe." But likely not.

"He might have been a crappy father and husband, not even much of a businessman, but he wasn't a criminal. Listen. As shady as this place used to be, and still is, in some people's eyes—"

"A *lot* of people's eyes."

"It meant the world to your dad, and to dozens of us. Jerks like me, but kids, too—teenagers, you know? If the gym weren't here, those guys would take whatever energy they pour into training and redirect it the wrong way. I know 'cause I used to be that kid myself, until my mom made me come here and your old man taught me about discipline and dedication. But it's nothing like it used to be. I'll show you every last corner of it. Every receipt from the past ten years, if you need proof. We've got nothing to hide."

She sank back in her chair, unwilling to be swayed by his little speech. Jenna was a softie at her core, a woman who sniffled during especially poignant life insurance commercials, sobbed through romantic movies and fell to pieces at weddings. But she'd uprooted herself to take advantage of the one taste of generosity her dad had ever bothered offering her. As tall and built and intimidating as Mercer Rowley might be, she'd prove herself twice as tough a competitor. She hadn't moved her entire life to this city so she could watch her bottom line slowly get eaten up by the floundering gym— the same way it had eaten up the child support payments her mom never received.

Mercer ran a hand through his short hair. "Look. I don't know you, and I don't know what you think goes on here."

"You're going to tell me it's noble, I'm sure. But I know it's more than that. A boy's club, for starters, no women allowed—"

"That's one of the things I'll look into, now that I'm the manager. And it's not that they're not allowed, there's just no place for them to change."

"How very welcoming."

"All it needs is a bit of rehab, to make space for a second locker room—"

She cut him off, shaking her head. "Save your breath. I know this place meant more to my father than having a relationship with his daughter, so I'm a hard sell, trust me."

His eyes widened. "Are you kidding? Your dad never shut up about you."

The remark felt like a punch to the head, spinning her around.

Mercer went on. "'Jenna's team came in first at the swim meet. Jenna got hired as a camp counselor. Jenna's going to college in Seattle. Jenna got a job on a cruise ship.'"

"Like any of that makes up for him not making any effort to be in my life."

His face flipped through a range of emotions, but no words passed his twitching lips.

"What? Go on, since you're such an expert about my relationship with my father."

His shook his head. "You're right, it's none of my business. But I love this place and I loved your dad, and like it or not, you're stuck with me, unless you feel like finding yourself a new GM."

Stuck indeed. It wasn't ideal, opening a dating service for successful professionals smack-dab in the entryway to a disreputable boxing gym. But then again, Mercer had a history here. He might prove a pain in her neck, but she was also turning his life inside out. He'd inherited this mess, same as her…but without the legal empowerment. It had to feel awful. She wouldn't convince him the gym needed a mercy killing any more than he'd convince her it was worth keeping open.

It was going to be an ugly autumn, but she'd better just accept that.

Her body had been tight as a fist, but she felt the grip softening, relenting. "We're not going to see eye to eye on this."

"No."

"And I mean what I said—I haven't decided for sure I'm closing the gym when New Year's rolls around. But don't…"

"Don't get my hopes up?"

"Exactly. I'm not trying to be a cold-hearted bitch. But I've seen the books. If things don't change, and fast, there's no justifying keeping the place open."

Mercer blew out a long breath, leaning back on the desk to blink up at the ceiling.

She pondered this naked display of angst from a man whose job it surely was to camouflage his emotions behind a wall of strength, real or affected. Before they met she'd prepared herself to be intimidated by his anger, but it was Mercer's openness that had her stymied. She glanced at his arms, at his fascinating, heavy-knuckled hands. Very odd breed, these fighter types. Her body warmed in a way that had alarmingly little to do with conflict.

Bad, bad, bad.

Romances were like candles. Lust was the flame, and passion the wick. Lust was important of course, but it was the practical compatibilities that made up the wax—shared goals, harmonious personalities, a healthy overlap of values and interests. The more wax you had, the thicker and taller a pillar you could make, and keep that wick burning nice and slow, keep the flame alive years after that initial spark.

With Mercer's body this close, she felt the scrape of the match head across the striker, but that was the end of it. An invitation to get burned. Nothing more.

"Four months," Mercer muttered.

"Four and a half." She hazarded a smile. "Hope you like a challenge."

He met her eyes. "I do. But this fight would be a hell of a lot easier if I had any control over the accounts and could fund even a few of the improvements this place needs to get profitable again. Your dad never even shelled out to have a website done."

"I noticed." If you looked the gym up on Google, eight of the first ten hits had to do with Monty Wilinski's criminal trial. PR was not on Mercer's side.

"If you're honestly willing to give the gym a chance during these next few months, I hope you realize change costs money. Maybe not a lot, but *something*."

"It's my intention to be reasonable."

Mercer exhaled mightily, seeming ready to put the argument to bed for the moment.

She softened her voice. "I think it's best for everyone if we keep this between ourselves. This whole trial period thing."

"On that, we're agreed.... You want a tour of the place while you're here? Quick look at your inheritance?"

"No, thank you. Some other time, maybe."

He nodded, seeming unsurprised. "You know, I forgot to say it, but I'm sorry for your loss."

His words tugged something in her middle, a pang of sadness she didn't know how to process. "Well, thank you.... I'm sorry for yours. It sounds like you two were really close."

"We were. It probably won't elevate me or him too much for you, but your old man was the closest thing I ever had to a father. Sorry he wasn't the same to you."

"Yes. Well." Jenna stood, trying her best to seem calm and businesslike, stern but not hurt. In her everyday life she wasn't stern or serious at all, but this place was far from the everyday. She had to keep her game face on, her dukes up, lest she back down too much with this man. If only she'd had training in such things.

She wheeled the chair back to its corner. "I'll come by and talk to you tomorrow, after I've gotten settled."

Mercer slid from the desk. "I'm usually around here someplace while the gym's open. If I'm not in the office, you can find me downstairs."

He offered his hand and Jenna shook it, thrown once more by the feel of it, rough and confident. *Rough and confident.* She felt a shiver, a little show of approval from a lamentably primitive bit of her female machinery.

MERCER WATCHED JENNA exit and walk past the office window. He laced his fingers behind his head and exhaled a long, ragged breath.

Glancing around the office, he felt as though he were seeing the brick walls and worn furnishings for the first time. This building might have saved his life as a teenager, drawing him away from the choices that had gotten his best friend killed and landed a few others on a path straight to prison. It'd been the only constant he'd known in a life full of endless moves and evictions and instability, the place where his angry, volatile butt had been put in its place, where he'd learned being strong had jack-shit to do with acting tough.

He'd see the gym close over his dead body.

But four months wasn't going to cut it. If he could get Jenna to agree to postpone the execution, maybe through the next year... An extra twelve months to start turning things around could make all the difference. There was a tournament fast approaching, and if all went well, a couple of their homegrown fighters could land pro contracts as a result. That would boost membership. They could shed a bit of their black-sheep rep as an old-school boxing gym gone to seed, and start proving they were an up-and-coming force to be reckoned with in the MMA scene.

But that was a big-ass *if*.

And if Jenna's word was any good, she'd maybe approve a few hundred bucks here and there to replace old equipment, but for a contractor to build a women's locker room, for serious advertising, for anything that'd bring in enough new members or the sponsorship to drag them out of the red...? Yeah, right.

Mercer needed some aspirin—Jenna was promising to be a royal pain in his ass. If a rather good-looking one.

And she looked roughly how he'd expected. More stylish, maybe. More grown-up. And sure, she was hot—sort of uptight, college-grad hot, and way out of Mercer's league. He wondered what Rich would make of her. Then again, his shameless right-hand man would hit on a fire hydrant if you perched a nice enough wig on it.

Mercer—and more than a few of his fellow fighters—had held theoretical candles for Jenna. Monty had spoken about her often and flashed her latest school portraits around, and she was like a celebrity inside these walls. Mercer had built her up as some exotic creature, his mentor's mysterious daughter off in California, moving to college in Seattle, living some exciting West Coast life, all blue eyes and pink cheeks, shiny brown hair, like a girl from a TV show.

He'd heard nothing but praise about her from Monty since he'd been a teenager, and he'd always assumed they were close, or at least *speaking*. It wasn't until the man was dying that he'd confessed to Mercer how much he regretted the way he'd treated Jenna's mom when they'd still been together, and how deeply it broke his heart that he and his only child had been out of contact for twenty-five years. Nearly her entire life.

Emotional crap had never been Mercer's strong suit, and Jenna made him feel way too many things for his comfort. Threatened, fascinated, confused, annoyed. Plus a strong and completely inappropriate attraction—like the AC had broken, the office suddenly filled up with muggy August heat.

He shook his head, banishing all that sultry bull. There were pressing crises that demanded his focus, thanks to Jenna Wilinski.

He'd been living for free in the apartment upstairs since Monty had gotten really sick and needed assistance, but it was doubtful Jenna would be eager for him to stay. And if they were stuck splitting the bottom floors between two mismatched businesses for the next few months, he ought to avoid stepping on her toes whenever possible.

Mercer had absolutely no issue being pitted against someone, provided that someone was his physical match. Could even be a man six inches and fifty pounds bigger than Mercer, no problem. Bring it on. But this…

He was used to proving himself with fists and knees and elbows, not the business acumen he frankly didn't possess, despite the title he'd grudgingly inherited. He was a trainer, not a general manager. Not an accountant or promoter or a secretary, though all those jobs had fallen to him since Monty had passed. Why the old guy had thought Mercer was up to the challenge, he had no clue. Monty had always given him more credit than he deserved, and in the ring it was a pressure he'd relished. But this just sucked.

He was up against a woman, a stranger beloved by the man Mercer had considered his own father. The conflict weighed heavily on his heart, confusing and complicated, not a dynamic he knew how to process. Nothing so simple as stripping down and climbing into a ring to let his fists do the proving.

Though it didn't change one fact—nothing got Mercer's blood pumping quite like a good fight.

2

JENNA RETURNED THE NEXT MORNING. Her gaze panned the foyer once more, but the uncertainty of the coming months cast her daydreams in shadows. She'd barely slept at the hotel, tossed around between excitement about her new venture and dread regarding the one she'd been saddled with…and some other curious, confusing feelings about the man at its helm.

The office was locked and dark, so she had no choice but to head for the wide set of steps in the rear and search for Mercer in the gym. She glanced at her clothes, one of a dozen new outfits she'd bought, needing a wardrobe that said *competent young business owner*. Clothes that might convince a professional man or woman to trust Jenna with their love life, though the choice would probably look stuffy and prim to a concrete basement full of blood-lusting boxers. Her new neighbors, for better or worse. Her new *employees* until the New Year arrived. Thank goodness their management was Mercer's territory.

She descended the steps, and the stairs doubled back at a landing with a watercooler and a framed vintage fight poster, *Marciano v. Walcott*. What struck Jenna first was the smell. Sweat. Rubber and leather. Disinfectant. The odd, pungent potpourri of her father's legacy. Not a fragrance that softly whispered *blossoming romance!* But a well-placed fan could probably keep it from wafting into the foyer.

The sounds came next, slapping and grunting and the squeak of equipment joints. Jenna took a final breath and stepped through the open double doors and into the gym.

It wasn't quite what she'd expected—not the shadowy, smoke-clouded drug-and-gambling den old newspaper articles had so vividly conjured. Roomier, brighter, even orderly. But the rest was as she'd imagined.

A dozen fighters worked out at punching bags and on mats. A pair of men in one of two elevated rings carried on a practice match, tapping one another, not hitting. Her heart hurt, as she'd expected it might.

There was something about fighting she found upsetting. A sport that put so much emphasis on the physical—on hurting people—and whose glory went to individuals. Jenna believed deep in her heart that people needed each other. They needed family and friends and partners and teammates, support systems and tribes. At the end of the day, fighting was about establishing who was the best, standing triumphant in some sweaty ring with your fist in the air, the loser cast aside, all alone.

Jenna had always gravitated to the opposite. As a teen she'd been a camp counselor during the summers, in charge of building communities out of groups of nervous strangers. In college she'd majored in social psychology and enjoyed it, but all the theorizing in the world didn't give her a fraction of the satisfaction that working with actual people did. In the end, she'd proudly framed her diploma and abandoned her intentions of becoming a therapist in favor of taking a job on a cruise ship as activities director. She was great at that stuff— bringing people together.

She looked around the gym. *It's a lonely sport,* she thought.

For lonely, distrustful people. Give her a softball league, any day.

It was looking as if she'd come down into this gloomy den for nothing, that Mercer wasn't here, that she'd have to come back later and feel this awfulness all over again—

"Hook, hook, hook!" The voice jerked her head to the left.

Mercer was shouting at a beefy young man, who dutifully doled out the punches he was ordered, thwacking the padded targets Mercer held between them. Both were shirtless, Mercer as pale as his student was dark, as lean as the young man was bulky. Jenna got distracted by Mercer's body. Like his nose, like his knuckles, his bare torso was fascinating, attractive in a way that made her wince. She'd never seen a man's body quite like his, toned and utterly stripped of fat. Efficient and dangerous. Her own body stirred, but surely that was just a weird chemical reaction, panic about being down here mixed with airborne testosterone or something.

As she approached, she donned her best impression of an unaffected, professional businesswoman.

"Mr. Rowley."

Once a fresh punch landed, Mercer dropped his guard to turn to her. "Jenna, hey." He spoke to his trainee. "Ten minutes on the rope, then go through those flexibility drills from yesterday."

The young man nodded and let the two of them be.

"Glad you came by." Mercer slipped the pads from his hands and set them aside, recinching the drawstring of his warm-up pants. "Bet you've been doing a lot of thinking. Should I be hopeful or terrified about this visit?"

She nearly smiled at that. "Pragmatism's probably wisest. Could we talk someplace less…"

"Feral?"

She nodded.

"Sure. Can you spare five minutes so you don't have to smell me?"

"Yes, of course."

"I'll meet you upstairs." He jogged to the locker room. Jenna watched as he went, surprised by how many muscles comprised the human back.

She loitered in the ground-floor entryway, pretending to browse the equipment case until Mercer came trotting up the steps, dressed in a T-shirt and different pants.

He unlocked the office. "Thanks for waiting."

Jenna followed him inside, noting his wet hair and a clean, manly smell—soap or deodorant. She sat in the guest chair, thinking this would be her future clients' view as they awaited her guidance with their romantic goals. Maybe her own Mr. Right would make an appointment in the coming months, walk across this very floor, take a seat before her and suck the breath straight out of her lungs. Okay, maybe not months… not given her track record. Sure, it sounded bad, a matchmaker not being lucky in love. She could admit that. But she wasn't afraid of commitment or anything. Just cautious. People could stand to be a bit more cautious, a bit more *logical,* when choosing a partner. Her mom sure could've been, back when she'd hooked up with Monty Wilinski.

Mercer sat on the desk, clasping his hands between his knees. "So, what's going on in that brain of yours? Prepared to give us Neanderthals a fair shake?"

"Yes, I am. My father cared about me enough to leave me this place. The least I can do is offer you guys a chance to prove me wrong. And as much funding as I can reasonably spare."

He sighed his relief. "Thanks."

"No need to thank me. It's not like I had much choice."

In her periphery, she sensed gym members crossing the foyer. She just hoped her future clients wouldn't be too put off by the curious human traffic marching past the office windows. To say nothing of the franchise standards overseer. She made a mental note to have said windows frosted.

"Well, I'll take grudging tolerance, if that's all I'm likely to get." Mercer leaned forward and they shook once more.

"I ought to warn you," he added, "the next month or so's going to be chaotic. You'll be moving in, plus there's a big mixed martial arts competition arranged for the first week of October."

Jenna nodded. She knew her father had switched the gym from straight boxing to include kickboxing and other disciplines in the past decade.

"Your dad sank a bit of money into it when the proposal first came up, to get our name on the event," Mercer went on. "We've been co-planning it for over a year with a few other Massachusetts gyms and a promotions outfit. We've got a few guys who're training their hearts out for it. I'm coaching a kid whose career it could launch." Pride warmed his voice and brightened his eyes, softening his fight-roughened features. "People are going to be really keyed up, so apologies in advance if my head's all over the place."

"Understood. Is it taking place here? Downstairs?"

He laughed. She hadn't heard him laugh before. It did something odd to her middle, the sound seeming to hum low and hot in her belly. *Oh dear.*

"No, not here," he said. "It'll be at an arena outside the city. Have you never watched any UFC?"

Any what? "No."

"Well, ours isn't a UFC event, but it's the same idea, and still a pretty big deal. Got a couple important names on the card, and scouts coming from the major organizations, looking for the next generation of pros. We're hoping for five thousand people."

"Whoa."

"Not much by Vegas standards, but not shabby, either. I'm hoping it'll be just the shot in the arm this place needs to finally shrug off its lousy rep, earn some due respect and attract new members. Turn those books around," he added pointedly.

"I'll have my fingers crossed for you, then."

"You should come. See what it is your dad helped start."

She cooled at that. "Maybe."

"Jenna?"

She raised her brow.

"Is there any chance I can talk you into extending the gym's…you know. Trial period? Through next year, or even just through the spring?" The sincerity in his eyes broke her heart a little.

"Unless something amazingly encouraging happens, I can't, no. Not without risking bankrupting both businesses."

"I figured you'd probably say that." After a disappointed huff, he slapped his thighs and met her gaze. "Couldn't hurt to ask."

Primary mission tackled, Jenna turned her focus to a more awkward one. "I need to see the apartment." The apartment where her father had lived since he'd walked out on Jenna and her mom. She'd been dreading this, having to sort through his things and confirm exactly how much of a stranger he was to her. "Do you have keys to it?"

"I do. And I already took care of your dad's stuff."

"Did you?" She bit her lip, torn between relief and annoyance.

He nodded. "I wound up moving into the spare room about nine months ago, when he was getting really bad."

"Oh. So you're still living there now?"

"I am. But needless to say, my name's not on any lease, so never fear, I'll vacate the second you say the word. I'm sure you're eager to get that place rented out to a paying tenant."

"And you got rid of all my dad's things?"

"Not all of them. But he asked me to do that, in the run-up to…you know. So you wouldn't have to."

So her father had trusted Mercer with his possessions, as well as his business. To spare Jenna the burden, ostensibly, but she couldn't help but feel she'd been excluded. She'd been left nothing but property and papers and account numbers, impersonal gifts, nothing imbued with a father's affection for his daughter.

Though what had she expected, really?

"He'd already started giving stuff away toward the end," Mercer went on. "To the guys he's trained over the years. I didn't touch the really sentimental things, pictures and books and letters. I thought you might want to go through that yourself."

"I would, I guess."

"He had a lot of photos of you, you know."

A sensation like a cold breeze tensed her. "No, I didn't know."

"Your mom must have sent them."

"I doubt that." *Never in a million years.* "My grandma, maybe."

"Well, he had tons of them. There's a big picture of you from some graduation, hanging right over the sofa."

Too many emotions surged through her, bringing tears she wouldn't shed in front of this stranger. "It was thoughtful of you to take care of that," she said tightly. "I'd like to move into the apartment, if it suits me." And seeing that it was free, she knew it would. "But I didn't realize anyone was living there."

"Squatting now, technically."

"Only technically." She warmed a little toward Mercer, grateful he was turning out to be a reasonable guy in the face of her showing up with plans to upend his livelihood. She'd return the favor. "I won't ask you to move out until you've got something lined up. Maybe two weeks? By September first?"

"I'd appreciate that. You want to see the place now?"

"Sure."

Mercer locked the office behind them and led Jenna to the back, through a door beyond the steps to the gym and up a flight to the second floor. Doing her best to ignore the flex of his shoulders under his T-shirt, she followed him down a hall toward the front of the building, where he unlocked the apartment—one dead bolt among several. Not the best omen for the neighborhood, but she'd heard repeatedly that Chinatown was on its way up. She could be a part of that, start fading the ugly mark her dad had left. Her branch of Spark could be a great addition to the swanky new tapas bar and upscale florist that also shared the huge, block-long building.

The door opened into a high-ceilinged living room, the far end drenched in noontime sunlight from the tall windows. The furniture was sparse and dated, but the raw space was an interior decorator's dream.

She looked to the wall above the couch, where a large framed photo of her hung, a flashback to her high school graduation. She quickly glanced away. "It's what, twelve hundred square feet?"

"Maybe not even that, but two bedrooms, nice kitchen if you remodeled it. Laundry, great storage."

Jenna was already itchy to get to work on this place. Her first apartment, all to herself... A thought occurred to her, surely too complicated to even consider negotiating. Yet her mouth burst out with, "Can I see the spare room?"

"I guess your dad's room is the spare room now."

"My dad's room, then."

He led her past a big combination kitchen and dining room that was begging for new appliances and a fresh coat of paint. Then Mercer's back drew her eyes again, that interesting shifting of muscle behind taut cotton.

He pushed in the door to a modest bedroom, bare except

for a bed frame and dresser. Its window opened onto a fire escape, facing an intersection and the garish sign for a Thai restaurant. An interesting view, but not one conducive to privacy or peace. She looked around, taking in the squares where posters or picture frames had preserved the slate-blue paint on three walls, brick comprising the final one.

She turned to Mercer. "Was this always his room, do you know?"

"I couldn't tell you for sure, but the last few years, at least. Is that too weird?"

"I don't know. He's basically a stranger to me." She'd expected to feel something stronger, standing inside these walls, but so far she felt only detached curiosity.

"Want to see the other room? In case it's more to your taste?"

She nodded and followed him to the far side of the apartment. The second room was furnished, neat but small, with a similar street view. Next door was the bathroom, also tiny.

"Everything's been retrofitted as residential, obviously," Mercer said. "And before the condo boom, so kinda wonky and half-assed—like the gigantic living room and kitchen and the closet-sized everything else. It's actually a toss-up which is bigger, my room or the pantry."

She perked at the notion of having her own pantry. "I don't mind. Makes it interesting. How's the neighborhood?"

"Willing to admit you're in Chinatown yet?"

She smirked. "Sure."

He leaned against the bathroom doorframe. "It's not perfect. But a thousand times nicer than when I was a kid."

"For no rent, it doesn't have to be Beacon Hill."

"On the plus side, there's not much worth burgling from a boxing gym. And security's free between six a.m. and ten at night."

She peeked inside the cabinet under the bathroom sink. "What do you mean?"

"There's only about eight hours a day when there's not at least one trained thug wandering around downstairs."

"Oh, right." She straightened to smile at him. "How very convenient." For reasons not entirely clear to her, she found Mercer reassuring. Physically, maybe. She swallowed, her gaze dropping to his chest before she caught herself. Shutting the cabinet, she mustered the nerve to ask, "How would you feel if I moved in before you moved out?"

"And we're roommates until I find my next place?"

She nodded.

"It's your apartment."

"Well, I'm asking how you'd feel about it."

He shrugged. "I can put up with anybody for two weeks."

She looked down to hide her grin, shaking her head. She could sense him smiling back, feel his nearness as tangibly as sunshine warming her skin. Dangerous.

"And hell." Mercer leaned an arm along the doorframe and brought his face a little closer to hers, making something hot and unwelcome spike in Jenna's pulse. He smirked. "Maybe us shacking up together is just the chance I need to grow on you—change your mind about ruining all our lives."

Praying he couldn't see how his nearness had flushed her cheeks, she stepped back and pretended to inspect the shower. "It'll save me a chunk of change on a hotel. Just don't be insulted if I run a background check on you."

"Don't be disappointed when you discover I'm not a felon. Let me know if you need help moving anything. I'll mobilize the troops." He nodded to the floor to mean the men laboring two stories below.

"I'll get moved in this week, I imagine."

"You're the boss."

The boss. An intriguing notion. Boss to a small, inherited army of brutes for now. To a well-groomed team of assistants in a couple months' time, all things going as planned.

They wandered back to the living room and Jenna stared down at the busy street from the front windows. There was an Asian grocery store and produce stand across the way, flanked by a dry cleaners and nail salon. Not the most elegant neighbors on that side of the block. But she'd wow her clients with a stylish foyer refurb, maybe find some cool framed prints of Chinatown and play up the neighborhood's colorful history.

She turned to find Mercer's attention not on the view, but her face. In the sunlight his hazel eyes were the warm, brownish green of a ripe pear. His gaze was direct and unflickering, intense as a floodlight. It seemed as though he were reading her thoughts. For a long moment, they just stared at one another. Too long a moment.

She swallowed, gaze flitting from his bare arm to the shape of his chest, the stubble peppering his jaw, the curve of his lower lip. He mirrored the scrutiny, and in place of the casual calm he'd shown before, there was something else. Something…mischievous.

"I've got an extra set of keys down in the office, if you want them today." His voice sounded so close, and so cool and assured when that stare was anything but.

She nodded, banishing the hyperawareness fogging her head. "That'd be good."

"You okay staying in your dad's old room?"

"Yeah. I'll bring my suitcases over in the morning. If I can arrange to have a mattress delivered by tomorrow night, that is."

"Works for me. Any furniture you need help with?"

She shook her head. "No, thank you. I'll buy most of the stuff new."

"Gotcha."

She sighed, feeling too many things. Overwhelmed, elated,

terrified. Attracted, most unnerving of all. "Thank you," she said again. "I know it's probably not easy being this courteous to me, considering my bias."

"What choice have I got?"

"Because I'm your boss?"

"Nah. Because I loved your dad. And he loved you. So I have to at least pretend to respect your wishes, as much as they suck."

She laughed. "Well, I guess that'll have to do."

JENNA CAME BACK late the next morning, unlocking the door to her new apartment with the keys Mercer had given her.

"Hello?" She waited for a reply, but none came. Good. That gave her plenty of time to wander around in peace, before the awkward dance of cohabitating with the enemy began.

Okay, fine. *Enemy* was too dramatic a word. Mercer was nice enough, and he was too young to have been complicit in the gym's infamous criminal activities. It weighed on her, holding his fate in her hands. The uncertainty of the unmade decision loomed like a dark cloud. A big, dark, muscular, Mercer Rowley-shaped cloud.

She dragged her suitcases through the door, struck once again by the size of the living room. Big enough to add a wet bar or breakfast nook, a cozy little home office.... Too much to wrap her head around this soon, and besides, the franchise had to take precedence. All in good time. All in small, manageable steps.

Step one, she unpacked a bag of her favorite coffee and figured out how to work the machine on the counter. While it brewed, she wandered from room to room, making a list of stuff she'd need to buy. Big list. Moderate budget.

She'd lived on the cruise ship for ten months a year for the past six years, her room and board included. During the downtime between seasons she'd stayed rent-free with her mom and stepdad, so she'd gotten used to being greeted by a robust number whenever she checked her bank balance. Goodbye to all that. Still, this was what she'd been saving for all that time, even if she hadn't known it. A worthy investment—her new business, her first adult home. Something bigger than herself, a grand, exciting, romantic adventure. A *calling.* She could just sense it.

She covered the living room and dining area, thoroughly ogled her new pantry. Mercer had a single shelf stocked, mostly canned soups and vegetables, boxes of rice pilaf and similar bachelorish fare. Just add meat.

After nosing around the bathroom and her bedroom, Jenna came to the guest room. The door was closed and she knocked, just to be safe. No reply, she pushed it open, panning her gaze around her temporary roommate's tidy territory. A nice double bed frame. She wondered if that was hers to keep when he moved out. She liked his view more than the one from her father's window, and thought maybe she'd take this room when Mercer left.

As she went to inspect the open closet, she spotted something on the computer desk—a yellow folder with *Business Notes* scribbled on its tab. Frowning, she lifted the cover, promising herself she'd only peek at the top page.

Ten minutes later, she'd read half the contents.

It turned out Jenna wasn't the only one who'd made plans. The folder held a stack of glossy brochures from elite training facilities, with various offerings circled and starred, plus page after typed page of Mercer's ideas for improving the gym, even quotes from contractors. Most intriguing of all were two prospectuses from local colleges—one for a nutrition science associate program, another for sports medicine, along with their blank applications.

"Hey."

Jenna gasped and spun around, finding Mercer leaning in

the threshold, peeling a banana. She closed the folder and set it back in its place. "I'm sorry. I was snooping."

He shrugged. "Technically, it's your room."

"Maybe, but that wasn't appropriate. I'm sorry."

"It's fine. I forgive you." He said it in a lofty, joking tone of supreme and holy magnanimity, giving Jenna permission to relax.

She glanced back at the folder. "Looks like you have some big plans."

"That I do. No clue where the funding might come from, but eventually I intend to haul this place out of the gutter and into the twenty-first century. Or I had. I guess that's all in your hands, now."

That stung. Jenna switched topics. "And you want to go to school to be a nutritionist?" She pictured his can-laden shelf, thinking he could use a few pointers.

"I don't really know…just batting ideas around. But I'm thirty-four, which is ancient in this business. If I was good enough to be a serious pro, I'd have been told so fifteen years ago."

She frowned sympathetically.

He swallowed a bite of banana. "Nah, don't feel bad. Fighting was never about that for me. As long as I'm fit enough to keep sparring with the younger guys, and to throw my hat in for the odd amateur tournament, I'm happy."

Certainly fit enough, some troublemaking bit of Jenna's brain interjected.

"Tough life, being a professional. I may not be the smartest guy you ever met, but I'd like to preserve the few marbles I've got left." He tapped his temple. "Maybe figure out how to preserve my boys' marbles, too. That's where that stuff from the sports medicine program comes in."

"Your boys? Sorry, do you have kids?"

"No, no, the guys I train."

"Oh, right. What did my father have you doing, before he passed away? What's your job title?"

He laughed. "You make it sound like I've got business cards. But I was mainly a trainer, and your old man's unofficial assistant. I helped him with the accounts and organized events, handled some of the outside managers and promoters. All-purpose flunky. This place is my life, as pathetic as that might sound to you."

"It doesn't sound pathetic." Without thinking, Jenna took a seat on the end of his bed, then immediately regretted it. Was the move too familiar, or too much of a liberty, on top of nosing through his file? Or just too much contact with Mercer's *bed?* It was too much of something. And her discomfort got worse when he wandered over and sat beside her. The square of comforter separating their thighs made a woefully flimsy buffer.

"I, um, I've got folders just like that one, for the franchise I'm opening," she managed to say. "It's not pathetic at all." *And maybe we're not so different, deep down.*

"Working with the young guys is great, but I'd love to learn more about the science behind it all, too. Maybe get certified to rehab injured fighters. Branch out, make the place more than a gym."

"Sounds ambitious," Jenna offered, sad to know this man's hopes were dying, just as her own were blooming. The energy between them shifted, that lustful sensation deepening to something more tender. More vulnerable. She shivered.

"That was always a pipe dream, though. Especially since I'm stuck as the GM, now—not much time left over for implementing any of my grand plans, even if we did have the money." Mercer stood. "Sorry to startle you. I just needed to grab a bite before the noon session starts. I guess I'll see you around later, roomie."

"Yeah. Sorry again. For snooping."

"If it ain't hidden, it ain't secret, boss-lady. But thanks just the same for the apology."

"Sure."

Seconds later she heard the front door click and she released a giant, guilty breath.

"Smooth, Jenna. Very smooth."

3

WHILE SHE WAS out scrounging lunch the next day, a call on Jenna's cell confirmed her mattress and box spring would arrive in the afternoon. She moved sheets and covers to the top of her shopping list, checked her mapping app and memorized the short route to Macy's.

She felt back in her element as she stepped inside the store, with its perfume smells, its colors, its familiarity and civility. And bedclothes! She hadn't shopped for sheets since she'd been getting ready to move away to college. She ran her hands over the samples—smooth cotton, flannel, clingy jersey, sateen and its ritzier, pricier cousin, silk. She wondered what sort of man she might meet here in her new city, someone worthy of inviting to enjoy her new sheets. A silk man, surely. Or satin. What sort of sheets did Mercer favor, she wondered—

Her phone buzzed in her pocket, batting the dangerous query aside. She checked the screen, greeted by another heartening taste of the familiar.

"Hi, Mom."

"Hey, Jen! What are you up to? Is this a good time?"

"Yes, fine. I'm sheet-shopping."

They chatted about Jenna's initial impressions of the building and the gym, and her mother sighed noisily, a sound she reserved exclusively for whenever the topic of her ex-husband came up. "Just don't let this Mercer person bully you into compromising too much. Those types can be very pushy."

"He's remarkably civil, considering what a threat I must seem like to him."

Another sigh. Jenna could supply the unspoken words for herself—*he sounds much more reasonable than your father ever would have been.* But since his passing, her mom had finally found it in herself to censor her opinions on the matter.

"Well, that's a relief. And a surprise."

"Yes, a very nice surprise." And a very nice-*looking* surprise, Jenna added to herself. *Oops.* "He was actually living with Monty, up until he died." It always felt funny, calling him that. But he wasn't her dad. Her stepfather was Dad. She considered mentioning she was letting Mercer stay for the time being, but that wouldn't earn her any maternal endorsements.

By three-thirty she was back at the apartment with her acquisitions. The place was empty again, and dark, the sun behind the tall buildings now. She headed for a lamp and turned the switch, but nothing happened. She tried another with the same luck.

"Huh." She'd have to hope Mercer was working. Before she left the apartment, she tossed her new bedclothes in the washer and checked her face by the last of the day's light. She ran a brush through her hair, rolling her eyes at herself. Silly impulse. The fact that she wasn't bleeding from an open wound ought to impress the barbarian horde.

Downstairs in the humid gym, she found Mercer in trainer-mode once again, though luckily with a shirt on. Far less distracting that way. He was observing some of the younger guys working out on the bags, and shouting the odd pointer. He spotted her as she approached, speaking loudly over the hip-hop music playing from unseen speakers.

"Heya, boss. How you doing?"

She had to admit, he was awfully nice. Awfully polite and accommodating, considering her intentions for his beloved gym. Though he *did* have every reason to butter her up. She'd be naive to go misdiagnosing his kindness as anything too personal.

"I'm fine, Mercer. How are you?"

"I'd be better if this kid would quit dragging his feet." He nodded in the direction of the young man he'd been working with the previous afternoon. "I didn't introduce you guys yesterday. How rude of me."

Mercer shouted and swept an arm to beckon the man over. He put on a fight announcer's voice. "A-a-a-nd from Boston, Massachusetts, nineteen years old, two hundred fifteen pounds, De-e-e-lante Waters! Jenna, this is Delante—Mattapan's answer to a young Holyfield. Delante, this is Jenna, Monty's daughter."

She was struck again by the young man's size—broad and meaty, way heavier than Mercer, though three or four inches shorter. Jenna shook his hand, feeling hesitance in the gesture, a shyness in his averted gaze not evident in any other aspect of the kid. "Hey," he mumbled. His hair was braided into a labyrinth of cornrows, ending into two puffy tufts at the nape of his neck.

"What's feeling lazy, pigtails?" Mercer asked him.

A shrug. "Footwork?"

"Couldn't agree more. Go to it. I'll catch up in a few minutes."

Delante left them to head for another part of the gym and Mercer turned to Jenna. "I didn't ask you the other day, but what do you think? Is this place what you imagined?"

She made a grudging face. "It's different than I expected. Less awful than my mom and the old news stories had me assuming."

"Be still my heart." Mercer smirked, and it made Jenna's middle squirm pleasantly.

Wait. Were they flirting?

"What were you expecting?" he asked. "A meth lab?"

"It's nice, I guess. I don't have anything to compare it to."

Mercer's gaze dropped. "Mind taking your shoes off?"

"Oh, sorry." Just as she stepped out of her flats, she caught sight of a young trainee running a mop over the mats beneath a row of punching bags, sopping up sweat. *Note to self—wash feet.*

Another man approached, dressed to fight in shorts, barefoot, with fingerless gloves on his hands. He had longish hair and dark, aristocratic features, a Spanish prince with an aquiline nose and a raging black eye. He and Mercer clasped hands and gave one another matching shoulder slaps before they looked to Jenna.

"Jenna, this is Rich Estrada. Rich, this is Jenna Wilinski."

Rich smiled—an easy, deadly, sigh-inducing smile, and took her hand in his gloved one. His smooth foreign airs evaporated the second he opened his mouth. His accent was pure Boston sandpaper, even heavier than Mercer's. "Good to meet ya. You must take after your mom, huh? Your dad was a fugly son of a bitch, God rest his soul."

"Thanks?" Jenna said through a laugh, and released his hand.

"Whatcha think of your sweaty-ass legacy?" Rich asked, crossing his scary arms over his chest.

She glanced at Mercer, unsure if he'd shared her so-called evil plans with his colleagues and made her a basement full of enemies. Hopefully not.

"She's acclimating," Mercer offered, then spoke to Jenna. "Rich is fighting in that MMA tournament in October, and he's our resident Muay Thai trainer."

"Moy what now?"

"Your dad sent him to study kickboxing in Thailand for a year, when this place was transitioning from pure boxing to mixed disciplines. Our loss when he hits it big and leaves us for some juicy pro contract."

Rich shrugged, dismissing his credentials.

"Now he's the gym's great white hope for a bit of positive press."

"Great Colombian hope," Rich corrected.

Jenna smiled politely, fighting a twinge of angst to know her dad had paid for this man to travel and get a once-in-a-lifetime education—no matter how brutal—when she hadn't received so much as a graduation card from him. Still, no use letting the hurt take deeper root. She'd wasted enough time on that. Heck, maybe he'd simply wanted sons.

She gave Rich's body a brief assessment, hoping maybe he'd stir that heat in her the way Mercer did and prove it was just an indiscriminate, misguided lust, a chemical misfire brought on by their ridiculous physiques. Nothing. But a second's glance at Mercer's mere forearm? *Zing.* Damn it.

"I won't keep you," she said to Mercer. "But I can't for the life of me figure out why the lights won't come on in the apartment."

"Oh, sorry. I should have told you. There's a master switch right as you enter, bit higher than you'd expect. Stupid design. Throwback to when the place was slated to be offices."

"I better go. The mattress people should be here soon."

"Cool. I'll be up around seven or so."

Jenna bade the men a good afternoon and headed for the steps. She wondered what they would say about her once she was out of earshot. If they knew about her plans for the matchmaking franchise, they probably thought she was some silly fish out of water, a frivolous romantic.

No more silly or frivolous than teaching men to beat the crap out of each other, she decided. Both valid passions. Then she made the mistake of picturing Mercer engaged in his passion, stripped to the waist in a ring, gleaming with sweat, his face set with concentration.

Oh, bad. Very bad.

The delivery truck was pulling up as she reached the foyer, and before Jenna knew it, her bed was in place and made up with her new sheets and covers. The next step would be to find a supermarket, then get better acquainted with the kitchen.

An hour later she was unpacking her groceries, fantasizing about how she'd refinish the counters, what color to paint the walls, when the snap of the dead bolt pulled her out of her home-improvement fantasies. Mercer entered and waved from across the living room.

She mustered a smile to cover up the nerves he triggered. "Hey, roommate."

"Hey, landlady. Did your mattress guys show up?"

"Yup. You done working for the day?"

"I am." He pushed off his shoes by the door and crossed to stand on the other side of the counter, eyeing her new purchases—coffee grinder, salad spinner, her first ever brand-new set of knives. "Very fancy," he said, examining her gleaming French press. "Must get that from your mom. Your dad ate the same dinner every night, for as long as I knew him."

"Really? What?"

"Roast beef sub from this dingy Polish hole-in-the-wall. Even made me sneak them into the hospital for him, once or twice. Probably kept that place in business, single-handed."

Jenna turned her attention back to her groceries, peeling stickers from her produce, avoiding Mercer's eyes.

"Sorry. Is it uncomfortable, me talking about him?" Leave it to a boxer to read all her little cues. Probably an ace at poker, too.

"That's too strong a word," she said with a shrug. "Just weird."

"What's your mom like?"

"What did my dad tell you she was like?" Jenna countered.

"He never said much, really. Which just meant he wasn't crazy about her, but was too nice to say so. Talked way more about you."

"Yeah. I'm sure he had plenty to say, considering he hadn't seen me since I was four and we moved away. Since we talked maybe twice on the phone, the whole rest of my childhood." Awkward calls, both on her birthday if she remembered correctly. False and overly cheerful, like chatting with a mall Santa.

"Well, he was really proud of you, anyhow."

Jenna sighed quietly, deciding now was the perfect time to open the wine she'd bought. She held it up to show Mercer. "Would you like a glass?"

He shook his head. "I don't drink much when I'm training."

"Not good for keeping in peak condition?"

Mercer reached over the counter to pull out a drawer and hand her a corkscrew, giving Jenna quite a nice view of his flexing arm.

"I actually meant I don't drink when I'm training other guys, getting one of the kids in shape for a match. I try to set a good example."

She filled a tumbler, mentally adding stemware to her growing shopping list. A definite must, should she find the time to finagle a date of her own, off the clock. She shot Mercer a smirk. "And you think teaching your trainees how to beat people senseless is a good example?"

He returned her smile, the gesture making him truly, properly handsome for a moment. She caught herself fixating on the contours of his chest and shoulders beneath his T-shirt, those deadly—literally deadly—arms braced on the counter.

"It's strange to look at you," Jenna said, corking the bottle, "knowing my dad had a part in raising you."

"Do you have a stepfather?"

"Yeah. My mom remarried when I was ten. That's probably a big part of why I never got in touch with my father. My stepdad's a great guy. I mean, *he's* my dad."

He'd changed their lives, nearly overnight. Her mom had been a wreck up until then, depressed and desperate and always struggling with multiple jobs, overwhelmed by the stress of being a single mother. Then her stepdad had shown up, and everything transformed. Her mother had blossomed with a good man's affection and support, and for the first time in her life, Jenna had understood how essential it was to feel secure. Like you weren't alone. And it went far beyond some old damsel-in-distress refrain—her stepdad had transformed, too. He'd told them so a thousand times. He'd offered them stability—financially and in so many other ways, but he'd benefited just as much. *You're the family I didn't even know I deserved,* he'd said one Thanksgiving. It was as if all their jagged edges had fit together like joints, the whole so much stronger than its pieces.

From then on, Jenna had gone forth in awe of the Healing Power of True Love—cue harp music—as only an adolescent girl could. As it turned out, she was great at spotting matches. Three sets of friends she'd gotten together in college were now married or engaged, another two pairs happily living together. More than once she'd been approached by people she'd introduced as strangers the year before on the cruise ship, back for another trip and wanting to tell her they were still together. It hadn't occurred to her it might just be her ideal career, not until she'd chanced upon an article about Spark, and read that the business was looking to expand to new markets. And like a sign from above, she'd inherited this place, not even six months later.

She sipped her wine. "I always thought it would be an insult to my stepdad if I went looking for my biological father, having only been told what a jerk he was."

Mercer winced.

"He was really good to you, huh?" Jenna asked.

"He was. Hard as hell, but that's what I needed. That's what a lot of kids need. Somebody who'll hold them to a higher standard, come down on them when they screw up. Forgive them when they try to do right."

She nodded thoughtfully and the conversation lagged. Mercer disappeared downstairs, returning with a laptop and a pad and pen, and setting up at the dining room table.

Jenna took another sip of her wine and deemed it worthy of her first evening in her new home. The faded paint and the jumble of her dead father's furniture—to say nothing of the stray boxer in the spare room—would need to go, but she wasn't in too much of a hurry. Like the wine, Mercer's presence put her mind at ease. Though his body, it seemed, was doomed to put hers on high alert.

"Jesus," he murmured, eyes on his screen. "Eighteen hundred for a studio apartment on Comm Ave? You're shitting me."

"No kidding. I did a little research myself, in case this place didn't pan out. I've never paid rent before, and man was I in for sticker shock."

"Never paid rent?"

"I worked for a cruise line for ages, and it's one of the perks."

"Huh. What did you do?"

"I was the activities director. I organized cocktail parties and dances and things like that."

"Is that good training for being a…whatever it is? Dating agent?"

"Matchmaker. And it is. I planned tons of events for singles. And I've had official training, since I applied to be a franchisee. I'm pretty good at matchmaking. I'm *really* good at it," she corrected. "It's exciting, watching people you introduce fall for each other." The most exciting thing in the world…except perhaps for falling in love yourself. Jenna hoped to confirm that theory, someday. Yeah, fine, maybe her romances so far hadn't been as epic as she'd envisioned, but she had faith.

"Not much like watching people you train step into a boxing ring to meet *their* matches, I bet," Mercer said.

She laughed. "No, I hope not. But maybe you guys do dating differently around here. Guess I'll find out."

"You're from Boston, though, right?"

"Technically. But I don't remember anything from before we moved to Sacramento. Where did you grow up?"

"All over. Mission Hill and East Boston for a while, then Back Bay, before the yuppies invaded."

"Is your family still there?"

"My mom got pushed out when her building was turned into condos. She's in Brookline, now."

Mercer went back to his clicking and squinting and scowling, and Jenna got her ingredients organized.

"I'm doing a stir-fry," she said as she peeled the plastic from her new cutting board. "Should I make enough for two?"

His chair squeaked and he wandered back to the counter. "If you're genuinely offering, sure. But I can make my own dinner if you're only being polite."

She glanced up, just long enough to get caught in that unwavering stare. "I don't mind. It's just as easy to cook for two."

"Okay, then."

Jenna decanted a slew of new spices into matching bottles, and as she opened a sack of rice she asked, "How hungry are you?"

"Hungry."

The proclamation gave her a fresh shiver, a silly stirring

of her libido she'd be wise to ignore. She measured enough brown rice for three people and got it simmering, checked the time and oiled her new wok. While the rice cooked, she set to work slicing vegetables and chicken. Mercer watched her hands with unhidden interest.

"I feel like I'm hosting a cooking show."

"It's fascinating."

"I gather you don't cook much, judging from what you think passes for staples in the pantry."

"Casualty of my upbringing. My mom was never home so I grew up on microwave meals and takeout. But when I moved to Brazil I realized I actually have a palate. And that foods that aren't beige and deep-fried taste pretty good, and make me a better fighter."

"Brazil?"

He nodded. "Your dad sent me there to study jujitsu for a year, when it was becoming clear that MMA wasn't a fad. Same idea as when Rich went to Thailand. He wanted us to bring back what we learned and incorporate it in the workouts. I'd prefer to get a proper, full-time jujitsu trainer on staff, but we can't afford it at the moment."

Jenna frowned to herself. *Two* men her father had paid to send abroad. Still, she'd been lucky to grow up with an amazing father figure. Mercer didn't seem to have had such a privilege built into his home life. She steered the topic back to food. "So my father didn't instill nutrition as part of your training?"

He laughed. "Nah. Monty was a red-meat-and-cigars kind of old-schooler. He barked a lot about carbs when we were bulking up or slimming down for a weigh-in, but that was the extent of his dietary advice. What's that?" He pointed to the vegetable she was chopping.

"Bok choy."

"And that?"

"That's a ginger root. If you feel like being useful," she

added, handing him a cheese grater and sliding a plate across the counter, "you can shave me a little pile of it. A teaspoon or so."

He tore away the grater's packaging and got to work. "Whew, there's a smell."

"Nice, isn't it?"

He took a deep whiff. "Actually, yeah."

She could feel herself relaxing, perhaps from the wine, perhaps from managing to see Mercer as something simpler than a partner or roadblock, or a rival for her father's love. As a friend, maybe. In time, if temporarily. She hoped so—it'd make working with him far easier, and soften the blow when she inevitably had to end the gym's suffering.

"Can I give you some cash for this stuff?" he asked.

"If you do end up helping me move furniture, this is the least of what I owe you." She drained her glass and poured herself a couple extra ounces. "You sure you don't want any of this? It's very good."

Mercer kept his attention on the grater and sighed dramatically. "You women. Evil temptresses."

"Is that a yes?"

He shook his head. "This is why I tell my kids to stay away from girls when they're training. Chicks and alcohol— nothing but trouble."

She could feel another seed of flirtation sprouting, changing the atmosphere between them. "Do you have a girlfriend?"

"No way. You're all more hassle than you're worth."

She stopped chopping to shoot him a look. "Remind me not to use that quote for the men-seeking-women section of my future website."

He grinned. "If I had a fight coming up, I'd opt for a broken rib over a clingy girlfriend. No contest which is more crippling."

"Now that's just *mean*."

"Nah, it's just true. You're distracting. With all your worrying and your phone calls and your…shapely parts." He shook his head as if trying to clear it of a feminine mind-control spell, and the flirtation seed officially put down roots.

"Guess I won't be signing you on as a client."

"Save that nonsense for the reformed frat boys cluttering up State Street. If you're too busy or lazy to go out and find a woman for yourself, you're probably too busy or lazy to keep her happy."

Jenna took a deep breath and asked a question that had been irking her since she'd snooped through his folder. "What do you think you'll do, when the gym closes?"

"Not even going to soften that with an 'if,' huh? Well, I'll probably go to work for another place, as a trainer."

"That doesn't sound too bad. And it might be better for your career, working somewhere a bit more reputable. Somewhere with more Google hits for its fighters' accomplishments than its criminal scandals."

Mercer made a face, looking as though he were smelling something far more pungent than ginger. "Doesn't sit right, working someplace else. Guys like me are loyal, sometimes to a fault, and it'd feel like I was spitting on everything your dad ever did for me."

She let one of his words bounce around in her head—*loyal.* Territorial. Protective. A strong man, capable of fighting to the death for his family. Her cavewoman libido stirred anew, a pleasurable, ill-advised warmth blooming in her body.

She glanced at Mercer's arms as he picked strands of ginger from the grater. One of his forearms bore a bruise as big as a coaster, and she fixated on those knuckles again— pronounced and scarred. A phrase flashed across her mind— *the human animal.* She swallowed, wishing she could blame these thoughts on the wine. It didn't bode well for a matchmaker to let lust trick her into an infatuation with a self-proclaimed commitmentphobe. *Oh yes, very good instincts at work.*

Jenna got the wok heating. "Tell me about Brazil."

"What do you want to know?"

"Oh, anything. I'm a romantic. Did you have any steamy love affairs down there?"

"I trained and competed for thirteen months straight, two hours' bumpy drive from the nearest real town. The only thing steamy for me in Brazil was the climate. Even if I'd had the chance, I'd have passed out from exhaustion on top of the poor woman."

"Aw, such a waste."

"Oh yeah. Cruel of me to deny the ladies of the world that famous Boston suaveness."

Jenna tossed the chicken and vegetables into the pan. A tad buzzed, she turned to scrutinize her roommate for a long moment, eyes narrowed.

"What?"

"You know, you'd be handsome if you hadn't been hit in the face so many times."

A slow, wicked smile answered her, and something flared between them, something hot and mutual, tangible as the heat rising from the stove. "Is that your idea of a seduction?"

She shook her head.

"Just as well. You should've seen me before the fighting. Way uglier than this. All the broken bones have done me good. Quite the face-lift."

She laughed.

"You know," Mercer said, "you'd be cute yourself, if you weren't hell-bent on wrecking my life."

Her face went warm from both aspects of his comment, and she hid her blush by tending to the sizzling stir-fry.

"So, Miss Matchmaker. You leave some poor guy crying back in California?"

"I was exiled on a ship for six years, remember?"

"And you never bothered hooking yourself up while you were helping all those lonely tourists?"

She shrugged. "I dated a few guys, sure. Coworkers, of course."

"Of course?"

"Well, there's no point getting involved with the guests, when they're only going to be around for a week. Which is fine for a fling, I guess, if unprofessional..."

"But you're not a fling-y kind of girl?"

"No, I'm not. And cruise ships are really incestuous places. You blink, and everyone's hooked up with everyone else— the lifeguard with the lounge singer, the nanny with the tango instructor. Sort of complicates a guy's appeal, knowing he's kissed half your friends by the time he gets to you."

"I can see how that might wreck the mystique."

"Plus the gossip on those ships is *shameless*. And I like that sort of stuff to stay private."

"Bit traditional, then?"

"Yeah, I guess you could say that." She offered a mysterious little grin and turned back to the stove. It was a curious sensation, knowing he was standing there, just on the other side of the counter. That life, that weird set of experiences and skills. And holy hell, that body. Jenna usually caught herself falling for tall, slender men. Mercer was tall enough, but slender...no. Not burly, either, but...*cut*. Yes, that was the adjective. If he ever wound up in her Boston bachelor database, she'd be stuck with the inadequate drop-down menu designation of *athletic* to qualify that build. And if Mercer was *athletic,* then Bill Gates was *well-off.*

"So, you won't be competing in that tournament next month?" she asked over her shoulder.

"Nah. I'm strictly there as Delante's corner. Gonna run that kid into the ground for the next six weeks." He grinned as though he relished such a chance. "Keep him too busy and too exhausted to worry about girls or any of the other nonsense waiting for him back in his neighborhood."

"He's like your project."

"I guess. But I don't do it for me. I didn't lose a year's sleep and nag myself hoarse to keep him from quitting high school because it was fun."

"Why, then?"

"You just see something in a guy. You can tell when a kid's got it, like this energy. He stands out. And you want to make him see it, too."

"And what did my dad see in you?"

Mercer laughed. "Hell, I dunno. I was never going to go pro, not big-time, and I'm sure he knew it. I think he just let me believe maybe I could, so I'd have something worth working toward, give me some direction. I guess he just liked me."

"What were you like, before boxing?"

"Pretty rotten apple. Or on my way there. My mom figured if her stupid-ass son was so hell-bent on getting himself in fights, maybe he could make something of it."

"Guess she was right."

He nodded. "Moms usually are. It's a tough age, fourteen, fifteen. You think you're a man, even though you're so incredibly not. If you don't know what you're good at by then, your identity starts latching on to whatever you're bad at. Whatever's got people paying attention to you. That's my theory, anyhow."

"I think there's some wisdom in that."

They fell silent, and Jenna felt that pleasant wave of nerves again. It would probably only last as long as her wine buzz, but she had a crush on Mercer. The feeling wouldn't be there when she woke, and their acquaintanceship was already complicated. They shared three key things—an apartment, a business and her dad—and tenuously so. They couldn't possibly add a romantic entanglement to that list and not expect it to implode. Still, why did Mercer's personality have to wind up being as appealing as his body?

"So, you don't really date, then," she heard herself asking as she turned down the burner under the veggies.

"Why, you need recruits for your harem?"

"It's called a client database. Are you just a love-'em-and-leave-'em kind of guy, then? Three rounds and tap out?"

He laughed. "For a girl who won't kiss and tell, you're awful nosy about other people's love lives."

She blushed. "Just the wine talking."

"Well, I don't really do serious relationships. Between my mom and your dad, I got a pretty thorough education in how much pain love can saddle you with, if you get it wrong. And most folks I know seem to get it wrong."

"That's why they need me," she said brightly. "To steer them in the right direction."

"No offense, but taking dating guidance from a single woman sounds like being taught to bird-watch from a blind guy."

Jenna gaped, playing up her offense. She grabbed a wet sponge and whipped it at him.

Laughing, Mercer batted it away. "Or hiring a homeless guy as your Realtor."

Scanning for a weapon, she reeled out the sink sprayer and gave it a quick, solid squeeze. Mercer studied the damp patch spreading down the front of his T-shirt, still chuckling. He looked up. "If you weren't a girl, my boss and my landlady, you'd be so dead right now."

The faintest smell of burning rice drew her attention, which was just as well—she was enjoying herself *far* too much.

"Get us some bowls, Mr. Rowley. It's time to eat."

4

THE WINE WAS TEMPTING.

Mercer stole a glance at Jenna across the kitchen. Also tempting. Also the worst idea in the history of the world, given the balancing act the next few months were going to demand. Plus she was into commitment and compatibility. Mercer wasn't a womanizer by any means, but he'd definitely spent more time in his cumulative flings than in a real relationship. He and Jenna played in very different leagues when it came to dating—hell, different sports—and matching the pair of them could only end in unintentional fouls and injuries.

Still, he could flirt. Nothing wrong with that. Might lighten the mood, break the ice, melt some of the tension that had marred their initial introduction…and turn the heat up under that other tension they had going on, which was far more fun.

"So," he said as they sat down at the table. "If I signed up with your little dating service, what type of woman would you match me with?"

"A fairly desperate one, I imagine," she teased.

"So I'm *your* type, then?"

She shot him a playful, killing look, probably wishing the sprayer were still within her reach. "Yes, very funny. But you told me yourself, you're not interested in a relationship. I'm not going to waste my time trying to find love for men who're only up for a random roll in the hay."

"I never said that's what I'm about. Not exactly."

"Anyway, you'd have to go through an exhaustive interview before I could figure out who you'd hit it off with. I barely know anything about you."

He took the first bite of his dinner, finally understanding why it might be worth going to all the trouble Jenna had. Beat the hell out of takeout. "This is delicious."

"Thank you."

"But go on. Ask me one of your dating-thing questions. Interview me."

She looked to the ceiling, dredging up a mental question-naire. How on earth was this Monty's daughter? She'd been putting on a semiconvincing tough-cookie act with him when it came to the business stuff, but beneath that thin shell she was a softie through and through. Mercer watched her shiny brown hair as it swung about her shoulders, wondering how it would feel wound around his fingers.

"Okay," she said. "Where do you see yourself ten years from now?"

He frowned, genuinely surprised to realize he hadn't the faintest clue. "Um, in a perfect world?"

"Sure."

"In a perfect world I'd still be here, running this place. But it'd be way different. All those things you snooped through and more."

"And…?"

"What else is there?"

Her fork clattered against her bowl and she gave him a supremely annoyed look. "You didn't even mention a wife or kids or any kind of personal life." She shook her head and resumed eating. "No way you're getting anywhere *near* my clientele."

"That's not fair. You tricked me."

"Didn't. Even. Register."

"Fine, stick a wife in the picture. I'd be a great husband. To the right woman." An exactly, *perfectly* right woman for him. There was no way he was taking a chance, only to wake up heartbroken or ditched, maybe miles away from a kid or two once the divorce dust settled. And if Mercer ever met such a woman, he'd know. Until then, no sense trying to make do with anything less.

Jenna rolled her eyes and speared a pea pod on her fork.

"What? I *would* be a great husband. Fix your car, rub your feet. Beat people up for you."

She laughed, shaking her head.

"Grill a mean steak, rewire your toaster. Great kisser."

"*All* men think they're great kissers. Just like you all think you're the only decent driver on the road."

"Maybe, but I am. Amazing kisser. Dangerously amazing. Your panties would, like, disintegrate, I'm such an awesome kisser."

"Uh-huh." Jenna seemed to bite back a smile.

"Don't act like that's not important. Like you've never been on a date and thought the guy was pretty okay until he went in for the good-night kiss and it was all…" He made a grossed-out face.

"It's important, but it's not everything."

"People should make out, like, ten minutes into a first date, and make sure that chemistry's there. If it's not, why waste the money on dinner?"

"Some people won't feel that with a person they don't know yet. Most women, I suspect, at the risk of sounding sexist."

"Well, that's what I'd tell my clients to do."

"You'd make a terrible matchmaker. And an even worse first date."

"Just leading with my strengths. I'd kiss you so good, you wouldn't even notice what a cheap restaurant I took you to."

She laughed again.

Mercer was happy to let the topic linger, enjoying flirting more than was advisable. But to his disappointment, Jenna changed the subject.

"Where'd you get your name from? I've never met a Mercer before."

"It was my great-uncle's name. He was a prizefighter in Baltimore, actually, back in the fifties. 'No-Mercy' Mercer McGill, he was called."

"Wow, now there's a name."

"Tell me about it. Lucky bastard."

"Do you have a fight nickname?"

"Nah. I was never a headliner. Decent record, though, brief as my semipro career was. Five and two, three knockouts. Don't think my odds were ever much to write home about."

Jenna went noticeably still, not speaking for a protracted moment. "There was probably tons of that going on. Gambling."

"Sure. Goes hand in hand with the sport, for better or worse."

"My dad must have been good at it…guessing outcomes."

There was bitterness in her voice, impossible to miss. Mercer felt it, too, her condemnation of her dad—hell, *his* dad, for all intents and purposes—putting him on the defensive. Nearly everybody believed Monty had been involved all those years ago, though Mercer refused to think him capable of it. Not the man who'd personally drawn him away from what would've surely been a similarly ugly path.

"Actually, your dad never gambled."

She met his eyes. "No? Why not? Was it forbidden if you're involved with one of the competitors?"

"Like that stops anybody. But no, he just wasn't interested

in that side of it. He thought it bred corruption and match-fixing."

"Huh." Her perplexed expression told him she'd been fed a much different story.

"Okay, actually, that was a lie," Mercer said. "Your dad did gamble on fights. Once on me, to win."

She relaxed, clearly vindicated.

"I won that match, think I got paid about five hundred dollars. Then your dad takes me aside in the locker room and tells me, 'Son, you just made yourself three grand. I'm sending you to Brazil.' He handed me this wad of cash and I was like, *excuse me?*"

"That's how he paid to send you abroad?"

Mercer nodded. "Didn't even know he'd been planning anything like that. Same with Rich. Made us both earn our way. Guess that's how he thought of it. Only two bets I ever heard of him placing."

Jenna seemed to mull all of this over as they ate, a crease of confusion pinched between her brows. Goddamned cute.

When they were done, Mercer took their bowls to the sink. "That was the best meal I've had in ages. Thanks."

"You're welcome. Nice to have the time and space to cook again."

He watched her out of the corner of his eye, her gaze moving restlessly around the apartment. Eventually she asked, "Do we have cable?"

"Yeah. Go nuts."

"Are you sticking around here for the night?"

"I was going to. Rich is overseeing the evening session. Is that a problem?"

She smiled tightly. "No, no. It's just that on Wednesdays I usually watch this show. It's really stupid, so I don't need to subject you to it."

"What?"

"This dumb dating show."

"What do you care what I think about your crappy taste in TV?"

"Fine. Just tell me if it's too loud or anything."

Mercer put the dishes in the sink to soak while Jenna got settled on the couch, messing with the remotes. He grabbed his notes and laptop and took a seat on the far cushion.

It felt funny—funny in a nice way—sharing a sofa with a woman. He hadn't had a date in a few months, thanks to Delante's increasingly high-maintenance training regimen. Felt good, sensing the soft presence of a female body. And not just any female body. The mystery girl he'd been curious about for years, who'd grown into quite a knockout, albeit a buttoned-up one.

The show started then promptly went to commercials. Jenna rose to get herself a fresh tumbler of wine. Mercer raised an eyebrow as she sat back down, legs folded under her swishy skirt, throw pillow hugged to her middle.

"What?"

"Nothing. Keep drinking and I'll trick you into thinking I'm charming."

She laughed, a tiny little huff through her nose. Pretty nose. Pretty mouth, blue eyes squinty when she smiled. He eyed the smooth, pale skin of her neck and the very tops of her breasts, wondering what it might taste like, and how soft it would feel against his lips, under his fight-roughened palms and fingertips.

She caught him staring. "Yes?"

"Just looking at you. Wondering how you dodged all your dad's homely genes."

"Was that a compliment?"

"Might pass for one if you finish that glass."

She shook her head, smiling.

"Polish off the bottle and maybe I'll pass for Brad Pitt."

A snort.

"You—"

She shushed him. "My stupid show's back on. Quit flirting with me."

Mercer waited for perhaps half a minute before he leaned across the center cushion to whisper loudly, "I was *not* flirting with you."

She sipped her wine, attention glued to the screen. "I know flirting when I see it."

"You're a hopeless romantic—" She shushed him again and Mercer leaned over even farther, so far he knew he looked ridiculous, practically lying down between them. He lowered his voice back to fake-whisper level. "You probably see flirting all over the place. You probably think those filthy hippies at Park Street with clipboard surveys are just interested in a date with you."

She turned to blink down at him, the cutest pantomime of annoyance he'd ever seen.

He sat up. "Fine. Live in denial."

Mercer went back to pretending to research apartments, and Jenna went back to what he assumed was pretending to watch her show. Ten minutes later, though, he knew she really was ignoring him. She made a disgusted noise.

"What?"

She shook her head. "I *knew* she'd pick him," she said, waving at the screen.

"Pick who for what?"

"Pick this hair-gelled personal trainer meathead for her getaway date, when she should have gone with the science teacher. What is *wrong* with these women?"

"As a trainer and a meathead, I find your outrage offensive."

She tried and failed to hide a smile.

"How can I sign you up for this show?" he asked.

"I don't kiss and tell. No way I'd ever let cameras follow me around while I made out with strange guys. Or worse! You should see the stuff that some of these girls will do on national TV." She sighed and sipped her wine.

"You drunk yet?"

"I've barely had two glasses. Why?"

"Nothing. Just wondering if I need to be worried. You get all buzzed, all worked up watching your little make-out show... You might try and take advantage of me."

Her lips tightened with a poorly suppressed smirk. "You think you're really cute, don't you?"

Mercer shrugged. Cute, no. He wouldn't be winning any beauty pageants, but after nearly twenty years of boxing, he could read other people's faces like billboards. Their emotions, fatigue, pain...attraction.

And Jenna's smirk told him everything he needed to know. The trouble was, he didn't have the first clue what to do with that information.

THEY DIDN'T SPEAK AGAIN until Jenna's show was over and a program about home decorating came on. She sat up straighter, thinking she might get some ideas for the apartment. Plus it'd be smart to force her mind off its awareness of Mercer's body, mere feet from hers. She glanced to the cushion beside him, at the pad he hadn't taken a note on since sitting down.

"Could I borrow that?" she asked, pointing to it.

He handed it to her. "Knock yourself out."

Mercer had written two headings at the top of the page— *Yes* and *Maybe.* Both were crossed out, and beneath he'd started a different list, one that included the items *Sell kidney* and *Rob a bank.* Thank goodness Jenna had landed an apartment for free. She didn't envy his challenge.

She flipped the pad to a fresh page and awaited the wisdom of the show's host, pen poised. But fifteen minutes or more passed and she'd absorbed nothing.

She kept thinking about what he'd said, about his supposed kissing prowess. Jenna hadn't kissed a guy—*really* kissed a guy—in ages. Polite smooches at the ends of a few first dates, but no deep, sexy, toe-curling kissing. She hadn't really given it much thought until Mercer had roused her curiosity, along with the dating show's on-screen lip-locking. She missed being kissed like that. Plus with Mercer, she might feel those interesting, scarred hands on her jaw, maybe run her own palms down his extraordinary arms. She blinked, waking from the trance. She grabbed the remote and switched off the television.

"Off to bed?" he asked.

"Yeah, I'm starting to zone out." She glanced at his computer. "Are you still depressing yourself with apartment listings?"

"Gave that up a while ago. Just catching up on some admin. Probably time I called it a night, too. I'm meeting Delante at seven tomorrow in Somerville. Gonna make him run the stairs in the Porter Square T station until his legs fall off."

"While you what? Sip a coffee on a bench?"

"Nah, I'll join him. Keep my own game up."

Again, she ogled his powerful arm. Bad. Bad eyes.

She rose and headed to the kitchen to clean up the dinner mess. She heard Mercer's laptop click closed and the couch creak.

"Don't," he said, walking over. "Let me do all that."

She opened the dishwasher and began rinsing the bowls. "I don't mind. It's still novel for me to even have a kitchen *to* clean."

He muscled her to the side and she submitted. "Fine." She turned instead to the items scattered across the counter, finding homes for her spices and new utensils. She nudged Mercer's unnaturally hard shoulder and he shifted to let her get to the trash can beneath the sink. She shut the cupboard door and stood at the exact moment he reached for her wineglass. Their chests brushed, faces inches apart. She felt her eyes widen, mirroring his.

"'Scuse me."

"Sorry."

Neither moved. Their eyes darted and she felt her lips part. His did the same. Unbidden, her chin tilted up, and Mercer's dipped in response.

"This is…" She trailed off.

"Yeah." They were so close, she felt his breath on her lips.

They were trapped, stuck in some mutual daze, mouths edging closer. She felt a warm, damp hand on her neck, heard the *clink* as he set her glass aside to free the other. She shivered at the rasp of his fingertips, then melted as his lips met hers. As she softened, he grew bolder, angling his head, kissing her deeply.

The hand cupping her neck was just as rough and commanding as she'd imagined. His tongue swept against hers, his kiss aggressive but controlled, and she felt consumed in a way she hadn't in ages. She grabbed his arm and the hardness there left her reeling. She'd never felt a kiss like this, never connected with a man on such a visceral, physical level, as if their mouths were made for one another, their bodies meant to join this way. Other ways.

But a voice was screaming in the back of her head, telling her to *stop, stop, stop.* Lust had slammed its foot on the gas, and if she didn't find the brake, they were going straight into a tree, a ditch, off the edge of a cliff.

She pushed firmly at his chest with both hands, and with a final deep taste, Mercer let her go. He licked his lips.

She took slow breaths, willing the madness to pass.

This man was too complicated. He was her employee, her

roommate. The son her father had wanted, a man whose very livelihood was at odds with hers. He was a dozen things that made this an awful, awful idea. But standing this close, the energy between them felt anything but complicated. It was a question with a single solution, and that solution was to feel his body against hers.

She grabbed his neck, and he was kissing her. She felt his hands on her shoulders, turning her, guiding her, pushing her lower back against the counter. His leg went between hers, driving her skirt a couple inches higher. He gathered her hair in his hands as she stroked her palms up his shoulders, his neck, cupped the back of his head and felt the soft bristle of his short hair. Between the deep strokes of his tongue and the press and tease of his lips, she heard his sounds—tiny grunts and moans. She imagined how much deeper and louder they'd be if they made a terrible decision and took this to one of the bedrooms…

No, no, no.

But as he kissed her, so firm and explicit, she knew this was hotter than any sex she'd had in the past five years. This wasn't attraction as she'd ever experienced it. It made her feel wild and helpless and electrified. So many things, all of them scary and exhilarating.

Mercer's kisses grew graceless and needy, and just as he seemed to be losing control, he broke away. The separation left Jenna aching. He looked drunk, his nose and ears and lips flushed, exactly where Jenna felt the heat. This insanity was mutual, and dangerous.

For long moments they stood that way, hands slowly slipping from one another's hair, breaths deepening, eyes locked on each other's mouths. Jenna cleared her throat, lust fading enough to expose a deep vein of embarrassment. She clasped her hands at her waist and felt blood flooding her cheeks, ashamed to have lost control of herself with a man she barely knew.

"You know, you're right." Mercer ran his tongue over his lower lip. "That's good wine."

She could think of nothing to say —no reprimand or smart remark or even a dumbfounded "Well." She closed her mouth and looked away. Mercer took a step back, then another.

The water was still running and he turned to the sink, resuming the dishes. Jenna pursed her tender lips, knowing she ought to say something. As she stowed the cutting board he handed her, she managed a weak "That was very… unexpected."

He shot her a teasing look, though a tighter, more cautious one than she'd grown to anticipate. "I suppose you're going to blame that on me?"

She mustered a weak laugh. "No. Wish I could, though." It scared her to know she was capable of such reckless attraction, so much stronger than logic.

"That was…that was a bad idea," she murmured.

"Probably."

"Definitely," she corrected, getting a hold of herself, smoothing her skirt and top.

"Let's just call that research or something, for your business."

She nodded vigorously. "Yes, good. I was just, um, comparing kissing data on East- versus West-Coast men. To better understand my new market."

Finally, another genuinely devious glance. "So how'd Boston measure up?"

"Bit more aggressive than I'd expected." Crap, they were flirting again.

"Aggressive, huh? How do you want to get kissed, then? All gentle, like I just took you to the ballet or a funeral or something?"

"I never said I didn't like it."

That shut him up a moment. "Well, good. Oh, wait, no. Bad."

She nodded. "Really bad."

"Really complicated."

For a few breaths they looked at each other with matching, perplexed expressions. Then Mercer said, "*Sort of* complicated. Or when you think about it, actually, it's really pretty *un*complicated. I mean, you'd never get hung up on me, since I'm like the opposite of your type."

"And you wouldn't get hung up on me, since I doubt you could commit to a sandwich long enough to finish it."

Mercer shut off the faucet and dried his hands on a dishtowel. "So really, that was a totally harmless accident."

Harmless, yes. Harmless as an alcoholic's first sip of liquor. She closed the cupboard. "Right… Well, good."

"Perfect."

"Yes, perfect." For a few moments, they shared a diplomatic calm, crisis averted. Then disaster struck, and Jenna couldn't for the life of her pinpoint whose fault it was when they were suddenly lip-locked again.

He was fiercer than ever, and she wasn't any better behaved. She stroked his shoulders and back, welcomed the heat and insistence of his tongue, the possessive weight of his palms on her waist and neck. They staggered a dozen paces to the couch, narrowly avoiding crushing Mercer's computer as he pulled her down to straddle his lap. It was dangerous how perfectly level their mouths were in this position. More dangerous still was how good his thighs felt as her knees sank into the cushions—hard and substantial. A hot palm pressed Jenna's bare, lower back, at the gap between her skirt and top.

She freed her mouth long enough to murmur, "This is such a stupid idea."

Mercer kissed her deeply for another breath before replying. "Yeah. Massively stupid."

But her body said it was pure genius, the thing she'd been put on this earth for. The only thing that mattered.

She held the back of his head, taking the lead. He massaged her skin, his other hand holding her hip, gently but unmistakably coaxing her closer. She obeyed, edging her center to his. Her skirt was gathered between their waists and she felt his erection through her panties and his jeans—hard as his arms and ten times as thrilling. His kisses faltered as he moaned, the noise giving her shivers. The strongest man she'd ever touched, totally helpless.

His hands went to her waist, guiding her in small thrusts against him. She leaned back and they both studied the scene, the point where their bodies met, his gaze rising to her breasts and throat, hers drawn as always to those powerful arms. He looked into her eyes.

"We should probably stop."

"Yes, we probably should," she agreed, yet neither put the advice into practice.

She leaned close again but the kissing was different. Mercer changed, distracted by the friction. His kisses were shallow, breath heavy. Sexy as hell. Though his hands still dictated her hips' rhythm, she knew he was at her mercy. She knew, too, she could have anything she wanted. She could run her curious palms over every fascinating inch of his exceptional body, issue any order and expect to have it followed. She could lead him by the collar to her never-slept-on mattress and christen the hell out of it. She could sleep with the gruffest, fittest, most shameless man she'd ever been attracted to and find out if he screwed as well as he kissed—

But no. No, no, no.

Jenna didn't *screw,* for starters.

She also couldn't sleep with a guy and not have it mean something. She'd wake up in deep trouble, unable to pretend she was capable of having sex without assigning significance to the act. Or scarier still, the fact that she wanted to have sex with Mercer meant she *already* felt something for him. That one was too much to contemplate. She shuffled back on her knees, separating their crotches, and flipped her skirt back down her thighs. "We really ought to stop. Like, really."

He nodded, the gesture looking hazy and crazed.

If romances were candles, as Jenna's philosophy suggested, then she and Mercer were a stick of dynamite. Nothing but a sizzling flame gobbling up the fuse en route to imminent disaster. They'd be over before her ears quit ringing. Then what?

A whole lot of fallout, that's what. A big old mess to clean up.

Good thing they'd managed to snuff things before it was too late. Her love life deserved to be as well thought out as her future clients'. And that meant observing one of the franchise's cardinal bits of advice—never sleep with someone before the fourth date. *Well done, Jenna. The man loads the dishwasher and suddenly you're on his lap.*

Mercer let her get to her feet.

She tidied her hair, caught her breath and did a very good job of not stealing a glance at the front of his jeans. Shutting herself in her room, she switched on the light and opened the window, welcoming the traffic sounds to chase the last of that impulsive lust from her consciousness.

Crisis dodged. Logic restored.

Then again, if logic was the main ingredient needed to make a lasting, passionate match, why wasn't Jenna still with her college flame? Or indeed her high school sweetheart? Two perfectly logical, perfectly likable men, but that hadn't kept her attached in the long run. Hadn't kept her up nights or left her pulse racing this way. She sat on the bed and rubbed her face, touched her lips, tender from Mercer's kisses.

Thank God in heaven she didn't have herself as a client.

5

AFTER THEY FINALLY, successfully separated, Mercer and Jenna had shared an awkward dance, negotiating the bathroom before retiring to their rooms for the night.

Mercer didn't think he'd gotten that worked up since tenth grade, and he entertained some rather unprofessional fantasies about his new roommate-slash-boss-slash-landlady before going to sleep. Still, that was safer than actually implementing any of his dick's many inspired ideas about what to do with the woman.

He woke up confused about the exchange, but resolved to let it go. He'd never wasted much time overthinking a sexual encounter before, and this was the last situation that needed overthinking. She was too many things to him, without also adding "crush" to the list.

He had plenty to worry about already, Delante first and foremost. He'd come under Mercer's tutelage the way Mercer had come under Monty's—grudgingly, shoved by a desperate mom at the end of her rope. That had been enough to get Mercer invested in the kid, but it took no time to realize Delante was special. A natural talent who thrived like a dying plant suddenly watered. Add the fact that the kid had a highly marketable projects-to-greatness urban underdog appeal, and Mercer knew he had something major on his hands.

If he could just keep Delante's head as focused as his punches, the guy could be signing a pro contract before the crowd had even filed out of the arena following next month's tournament. It was good for Delante, no doubt. Great for the gym, too—a boost right when they needed one most. Nothing fostered new memberships like launching a big name, and the boxers who'd come out of the gym in the eighties were ancient history. MMA was the future. Rich was rising in the ranks, too, a respected semipro with a lot of managers' eyes on him, but Delante was almost a decade younger, ripe for a long, enviable career.

They met early, and Mercer worked him into the ground, running and dodging commuters up and down the endless Porter Square Station stairs, until a T security guy told them to knock it off. They jogged the four miles through Cambridge and Boston back to Chinatown, greeted by an irksome sight when they finally reached the gym.

"Cool down and hit the showers," Mercer said, knowing he had to end Delante's torture earlier than he'd planned. Delante hauled his tired ass inside the building and Mercer stared up at the big plastic banner hung over the entryway, almost completely obscuring the gym's sign.

Future home of Spark: Boston! it proclaimed in a bold, modern font. *Your local branch of the Northeast's most respected dating service for busy professionals. Your perfect match is just a heartbeat away!* Below were web and email addresses.

Mercer read it three times, frown growing deeper with each pass. The businesses were cohabitating, sure. But it wrenched his guts, because the facts were plain. He had a single season to turn the gym around—the blink of an eye—and if the neighborhood knew the details, they'd no doubt be rooting for him to fail. For all he knew, Jenna was rooting for the same, all the better for her new venture's image. All the better that she get busy hiding the gym's very existence.

How easily Mercer had let himself forget what side she stood on the second they'd been tangled on the couch.

He jogged up the steps and into the foyer. The office was lit but locked, and he could see Jenna's half-finished lunch on the desk. He ran up to the apartment, but she wasn't there, either. Must have gone out on an errand.

He headed back to the gym, ditching his shoes and thinking he'd better find somebody down there to spar and work off some of his angst. Angst that felt distinctly like misplaced lust. Felt like way too many things. Feelings. Blergh.

And *feelings* promptly punched him in the face as he near-literally ran into Jenna heading up the steps.

"Hey," she said, her smile polite but nervous. Nervous because of the sign or because of them getting to second base on the couch, Mercer couldn't pinpoint.

"I was just looking for you," she said.

"I was just looking for you."

"Oh?"

He nodded. "We gotta talk about that sign."

"I know. I'm sorry—that's why I was trying to find you. The franchise people came to take a tour of the space. I didn't know they'd put that up so soon. Or, you know…quite so prominently. I didn't see it until after the men with the ladder had gone."

Mercer sighed, irritation lifting a little. One less emotion. Good. But there were still plenty underneath, all charged with that physical tension from the night before. Except down here…

Down here, Mercer could keep his priorities straight.

"That sign's going to cause a stir with the guys. I haven't told anybody the deal yet. But we've been needing new equipment for years, and suddenly there's the money to open an entirely new franchise? You're not going to make any friends that way."

She crossed her arms, and God help him, that defiant little gesture had his anger morphing to lust in a heartbeat.

"I'm not here to make friends. I'm here to run a business."

"Two businesses."

She was kind or smart enough not to add, *For now.* "I haven't forgotten that."

He glanced at her feet. "Take your shoes off. These mats have enough holes in them already."

She yanked off her heels. "I know it looks bad. That's why I apologized. But this place is your territory. Spark is mine."

"I can't have a bunch of keyed-up fighters questioning the future of this place so soon." It hurt too much to even know the score himself. "Not with an important tournament coming up."

"I get it, and I'm sorry. Like I said, I didn't ask them to put the sign where they did. Maybe we could find a ladder and move it up, so it doesn't look so…"

"Condemning?"

"Yeah." She sighed, sounding exhausted. "We'll figure something out."

"Yeah, we will. What's up with you, anyway? You look beat."

Another loaded breath. "It's fine. It was just stressful, showing the managers around, not knowing what they'd make of the place. It was approved last month on paper, but who knows what improvements the franchise overseer will demand to get it up to Spark standards. Or how much it'll cost. But they said they like the neighborhood—I hadn't been sure they would."

"And the neighbors?" he asked, jerking his head to mean the gym.

She smiled, a tight, apologetic gesture. "I won't pretend they were giddy about it."

"No, I'm sure they weren't." Suddenly exhausted himself, Mercer cast his gaze around, searching for a change of topic. A distraction from both the conflict and the attraction that had him so screwed up in the head.

"There's something I was meaning to show you, next time you were down here."

"Oh?"

He led her to the back wall. It was plastered with old boxing posters. Photos of the greats, newspaper and magazine stories about local fighters hung behind Lucite. He tapped an item in the middle and she came close to peer at it. It was a yellowed article from her hometown paper, with a picture of Jenna at age twelve or so, in a bathing cap and suit, holding up a medal for her team's showing in a county swim meet. He watched her face, her blue eyes widening only to then narrow, lips pursed in a tight line.

"He put that right up there, with all the stories about his favorite fighters," Mercer offered.

"Yeah. That's sweet." She was forcing a pleasant response, but Mercer couldn't even guess what emotion she was aiming for.

He pressed on anyway, compelled as always to defend her dad. "He was really proud of you. Never shut up about you."

"Great. Thanks for showing me that. It's very touching." She was so lousy at faking enthusiasm, she almost sounded sarcastic. Mercer felt suddenly diminished, reduced to a sweaty, weary heap of aching muscles. Maybe it had just been the wine for her, all along.

"Well. I'll let you get back to your work."

She nodded. "You too."

"I'll get one of the guys to help me with the sign. Hoist it up a couple feet so it's clear our two ventures are just cohabitating. And I'll get busy letting everyone know you're taking over the office and all that, for the dating thing."

"Thanks. Tell them they're free to ask me about it. If anyone's confused or concerned."

He smiled grimly. "I'll be first in line."

Her gaze jumped to the article he'd shown her.

"He was a good guy," Mercer said. "I'd prove it to you, if you gave me half a chance."

She chewed on a reply but swallowed it, unspoken. "See you around the apartment."

"Yeah. Sounds good."

Jenna began to walk away, taking Mercer's energy with her. Then she turned, and a little glimmer of her sweet self broke through the crust. "If you like frittata, I can make enough for two tonight."

He warmed at the offer, so tempted to toss a teasing remark back and remind her what happened the last time they'd shared a meal. "I'm not sure what that is. But if it's food, then yeah, that'd be real nice."

"Seven-thirty?"

"I'm leading a session at seven, but make it eight-fifteen and it's a date, Miss Matchmaker."

Finally, she smiled. And just like that, he was screwed. Two seconds' flirting and he wanted her again, worse than ever.

Shit. He better schedule himself a sadistic workout for the late afternoon. Better haul his body up those steps too tired to chew, let alone to muster the energy to mess around. Because near-high-school dropout or not, Mercer was smart enough to know that if Jenna couldn't manage to keep them strictly platonic tonight…he didn't stand a chance in hell.

When Mercer entered the apartment just after eight, Jenna stood a little straighter behind the counter, chopping peppers, steeling herself.

"Hey."

"Hey yourself, roommate."

He looked dead tired. Maybe just the by-product of a long, physical workday, or maybe he felt as beat-down as she did, following the unfortunate misunderstanding with the sign. On top of that, she'd spent almost the entire day in the office, and no less than twenty gym members had interrupted to express their condolences, most of them then regaling her with legendary tales of her larger-than-life father. Thoughtful gestures, though each one she smiled through had only reminded her how close he'd been to these strangers, to everyone but her. She felt as tired as Mercer looked.

After disappearing into his room with his gym bag, Mercer came to loiter on the opposite side of the counter. He eyed the bowl of egg mixture. "What's this called again?"

"Frittata. Not quite an omelet, not quite a quiche."

"I'm not entirely sure what a quiche is. So, how was your day?"

"Long. Spent most of it getting pummeled with all the stuff the franchise overseers are going to be sweeping through to do in the next couple months."

"Nothing like a good pummeling. What sort of stuff?"

"They're sending a bunch of people tomorrow, a design team to drop off the upholstery swatches and paint chips I'm allowed to choose from when I decorate my office. And some last-minute inspection stuff, technicalities before the space gets official approval."

"You need me to clean the gym's clutter out of there?"

"Not immediately, but soon." Jenna turned back to the cutting board. "How was your day, aside from that unpleasant surprise? Thanks for moving the sign, by the way."

"No problem. And my day was long."

"How were your stairs?"

"Also long." He leaned his forearms on the counter, watching her busy hands. "But whatever keeps the kid too beat to worry about bullshit back home, or worse. Girls."

"Right. No greater threat to you mercenary types than we ladies."

Mercer smirked.

As Jenna sliced mushrooms, she mustered the courage to say, "Speaking of the danger of women... The dangers of sex and romance, that is."

"Yeah?"

"I'm issuing us a mutual restraining order tonight."

He laughed, and though he was clearly confused, it was nice to see him really smiling again. "Pardon?"

"I think we should stay separated by at least four feet at all times. For our own good." Though even as she said it, she felt heat blooming in her body, felt her resolve turning soft and lazy.

Mercer seemed to consider the proposal, standing up straight and measuring the counter with his gaze. He took a step back. "About like that?"

"Yes. It just seems safer. Well, maybe *safe*'s not the word— less complicated."

"So, that means you still like me, even when you're not drunk?" A different smile, one Jenna enjoyed far too much.

"I was *not* drunk. And don't flirt with me. That's off-limits as well. I don't know what exactly's going on with us, attraction-wise. But no need to make it worse. No passing by each other in small spaces, no suggestive remarks..."

"No assaulting me with the sink sprayer?"

"Sadly, no. None of that stuff." She sighed, knowing that flirting their way around this topic wasn't going to do a lick of good. "I don't...I don't trust myself around you, and we're the last two people who need to get confused about who we are to each other."

"You feel confused about last night? I thought it was pretty straightforward."

She made an exasperated noise. "I'm trying to be serious for a second. That's yet another reason to be careful around each other until you move out. I don't work the way I suspect you do, with sex. It's very…complicated."

"Doesn't have to be."

She shot him a stern look, then went back to chopping. "I'm a pretty stereotypical woman when it comes to sex. It changes everything, emotionally, whether I want it to or not. You seem like a stereotypical man about it. If we did it—which we *won't*—"

"Noted."

"—you'd probably feel the same way about me the next day."

"And as a stereotypical woman you'd find that infuriating."

"Likely. Hence the restraining order."

Mercer crossed his arms and leaned against the wall. "You're right. You'd definitely feel different about me the next day. I'm even better at sex than I am at kissing."

She narrowed her eyes at him.

"Sorry. I'll quit it." He paused a moment before going on. "And I'm with you, incidentally. I think us messing around is a lousy idea, too. It's just fun winding you up."

Though she forced herself to nod and say, "I'm glad we're on the same page," Jenna felt a pang to hear Mercer agree. She knew in her head that made no sense, but a tiny, illogical part of her couldn't help but think, *How can it be terrible, when it feels so wonderful?*

They ate on the couch, the empty cushion between them taunting. So far, yet so close. Jenna found a news special on TV covering a very bloody civil war. If that couldn't kill the restlessness warming her body, nothing would. Sadly, she caught herself glancing Mercer's way every minute or two, remembering everything that had happened on that end of the couch, twenty-four hours earlier. Clearly, her attraction was more potent than violent overseas unrest.

Mercer had gone quiet, and stayed that way through the meal. He was rattled, and from what, she couldn't be sure. By her fessing up to the fact that there was no such thing as strings-free sex to her? Surely that would give a man like Mercer much-needed pause. Or perhaps from the simple fact that his entire life had been turned upside down in the past four days. By her. Also a distinct possibility, and an ugly one. Guilt soured Jenna's stomach.

When dinner was done Mercer took her plate, and Jenna honored their restraining order and let him do the dishes alone. Though she did steal a couple glances at his shoulders as he worked, those swells of muscle highlighted by the kitchen's overhead bulbs. Oops.

She changed into lounge pants and a T-shirt and cardigan and got cozy on her end of the couch. There was a pre-grand-opening client recruitment party to organize for mid-September, and now was the perfect time to fill her head with lists. Get her mind off the man sharing her home.

When Mercer finished cleaning the kitchen, he eyed her for a moment before announcing, "I'm gonna head downstairs for a little while."

"If I don't see you before I go to bed, good night."

He nodded, filled a water bottle from the sink and left, dead bolt snapping behind him. Jenna released a held breath.

She should have gone to bed at ten. By eleven, surely. Yet when quarter to midnight rolled around, she was still watching TV, barely taking in the program. She wasn't preoccupied by party to-dos, either. Her list was exactly one item long. *Hire assistant.* No, it was still Mercer, keeping her distracted, her feelings for him pacing low in her belly, a restless, reckless awareness.

But at twelve-thirty, curiosity became concern. Mercer's "little while" was now pushing three hours, and the gym was long closed for the night.

She grabbed her keys, slid into flip-flops and went down to the first floor. The office was dark, but the stairs to the gym were lit.

She heard Mercer before she saw him, the thump of his fist and the hiss of his sharp breaths. The space felt huge in the darkness, its smell mysterious, heady and foreign as a jungle.

Only the lights illuminating the row of heavy bags along one wall were switched on. Mercer was dressed in shorts, barefoot and shirtless, gloves on his hands. The bulbs cast him in harsh, dramatic shadows, his shoulders shining with sweat. The bag was suspended from the ceiling by a thick chain, and it jangled with every kick and punch, every knee and elbow he whacked it with. He danced from foot to foot, lost in his own world, in his imaginary battle.

Jenna's legs went wobbly, heat pooling in traitorous places. This man didn't waste any of the physical gifts humans were born with, every muscle honed and disciplined and punished, day after day, until he made violence look like art. That this workout was likely inspired by the angst she'd roused in him dampened her pleasure.

After another minute's assault, Mercer paused to grab a bottle of water from the mat beside him. Jenna approached.

When he set the bottle down, she caught his eye and he started. "Jesus, don't sneak up on me when I'm wearing these." He held up his gloved hands.

"Sorry. What are you doing?"

"What's it look like?"

"If I had to guess, you're working off how annoyed you must be at me."

He blinked, looking more startled than when he'd spotted her.

"We can talk about it, if you want. But maybe this is how you prefer to—"

"I'm not angry at you." He looked troubled. "I'm definitely not down here wailing on something because I wish I could wail on you."

"No, I didn't think *that*."

"I'm trying to wear myself out."

"Oh. Okay."

Three times he opened his mouth, poised to say something, only to close it again.

"What?"

He shook his head. "It'll sound like flirting and you'll chew me out again, so forget it."

"No, what?"

He huffed a breath through his nose. "I'm down here wearing myself out, so the second I put my head on the pillow I'll be unconscious. 'Cause if I don't, my brain's gonna be full of thoughts that probably violate some *mental* restraining order you didn't tell me about."

Jenna's turn to start. For a split second her mind supplied a vision of such a thing, of Mercer succumbing to fantasies about whatever inappropriate things he felt she was denying them. She shoved the image away. His body was dangerous and distracting enough, here in reality. No good could come of hypothesizing about the few bits of him she'd yet to lay her eyes—or hands—on.

With a huff, Mercer sat cross-legged on the mat. He ripped the Velcro straps from his wrists and tugged off his gloves. His hands were wrapped in white tape, and he ran them over his head, blowing out a heavy breath.

Jenna sat a few paces away, hugging her knees.

"Maybe I should just move out now," Mercer said.

"To where?"

"I dunno. Sublet somewhere, cash in a favor and crash on

somebody's couch till I find a place I can afford. It was nice of you to let me stay, but that was before we knew we're…"

"Allergic to each other?" It earned her a grudging smile.

"I know you think this is simple for me," he said. "Like I think sex is as incidental as a movie we might watch together. I wish it was. But you're my mentor's daughter. And the woman who turned up here prepared to end my life as I know it."

Unsure what to say to that, she kept her mouth shut.

"I dunno what the hell to make of you, Jenna. My body has plans for yours—plans I can usually take or leave, because sex doesn't come first for me, believe it or not. My responsibilities do, and you're the worst possible woman I could let myself get distracted by."

"I'm sure." She was spacey, lost in what he'd said about his body having plans for hers. She felt strangely honored to be singled out, maybe *targeted,* curious beyond belief.

"What I joked with you about in the kitchen was bullshit. This isn't simple to me at all."

Not sure how to process what he was telling her, she looked to his legs, to the red smear streaked along one shin. "You're bleeding."

He glanced down. "Oh, right. I've got no feeling left there anymore. No decent kickboxer does."

She laughed, shaking her head. "You're the strangest man I've ever met. Why don't you come upstairs and get cleaned up?"

A monstrous sigh. "Yeah, fine. I can barely move now, so my work here's probably done."

Jenna stood and offered him a hand. He clasped it in his wrapped one and she helped haul him to his feet. The cotton tape felt exotic against her palm, his hand big and scarred and fascinating as always. Allergic indeed.

She was ready to take her hand back, but he held it in his grip, his eyes on hers. "Why'd you come down here, anyway?"

"To see if you were okay."

"I really seemed like that much of a mess?"

She nodded.

"Better work on my game face."

He dropped his gaze and her hand, then wandered to grab his water bottle and shirt, slipped flip-flops on his feet. She tried and failed to keep her eyes off his bare chest and stomach and arms, that body looking as reckless as the urges it inspired in her. But they were in firm agreement on one fact—hooking up was a terrible idea. It nearly disappointed her. If Mercer had kept that door open on his end, she just might have let herself be yanked inside.

He hit the lights and locked up, and they trudged up the two flights and down the hall to the apartment.

She shut the door behind them and it felt as if something ought to be said. An apology tendered, or even a joke to lighten the heavy atmosphere.

"That's a really nerdy sweater," Mercer said.

She laughed, relieved by his levity but pretending offense. She looked down at her argyle cardigan. "It's librarian chic."

Neither spoke for a moment, though she knew he was struggling for the next quip, same as her. Words came, but not ones she'd expected.

"I don't want you to move out. I mean, I don't want you to feel like you have to move out sooner than we'd discussed."

"It might make everything simpler."

"It might. But I'm already turning your life upside down by even being here. You're acting a lot more civil about us coexisting than most people would, knowing what could happen come January. If letting you live here makes the transition easier, it's the least I can do."

He nodded. "Okay."

She sighed, staring at their feet, if only to keep her eyes off the more arousing bits of Mercer. Even with her gaze preoccupied, his scent was all around her, heady and exciting, as thrilling as a physical touch.

"This is going to be complicated, no matter what we do," he murmured. "No matter if I stay or go, or whatever rules we invent to keep from sexually assaulting each other, or how hard we try to rationalize everything."

She nodded.

"So it can't actually get much worse."

"Not that I can foresee," she said.

"Right."

She sensed it as he stood a little straighter, and she raised her chin to scan his face. He still looked beat, but there was a glimmer of resolution. He'd made peace with their situation.

"I'm gonna kiss you now."

She started. "Excuse me?"

"Things between us can't get any worse, so I'm gonna go ahead and make a move on you. Only way I'll be able to get any sleep tonight."

"Don't do that." *Do it. Do it.*

He put his wrapped hand to her jaw, leaned in and pressed his lips to hers. He kept it slow to start, giving Jenna a chance to protest, a chance to cling to her charade of propriety.

No way in hell.

She kissed him back, tasting salt on his lips—the flavor of a man who'd spent the past few hours trying to beat the desire out of his body. Desire for *her.* His tongue brushed hers and she grabbed his arm, thrilling anew at its hardness, its size. He kissed her until soft moans hummed from his throat, until he'd backed her against the door and her palms had slid south, from his chest to his stomach to his hips. Next and final stop—Bad Decisionville.

He broke away, taking a step back. The look in his eyes was wild and his tongue traced the corner of his lips. He began unwinding the tape from his hands, exciting as a striptease. Jenna held her breath until he spoke.

"I'm gonna take a shower. That gives you ten minutes to change your mind about where this is heading. If you come to your senses, shut your bedroom door. If you're as stupid as me, leave it open, and we'll find out what the hell else is supposed to happen between us."

6

JENNA WAS FROZEN, dumbfounded as she watched Mercer turn the corner to the bathroom. Ten minutes? Ten minutes wasn't nearly enough time to decide what to do.

Then again, ten minutes was plenty of time to change into cuter underwear, and wasn't that her answer, right there?

She jogged to her room and flung her suitcase open, rifling for anything that matched, preferably involving lace. Quick as a pit crew, she stripped and changed into her best bra and boy shorts, found a black camisole and yanked her pj's back up her legs. It'd be dumb to pretend this was any kind of smooth seduction, so she didn't bother wishing for candles, for a chance to freshen her makeup. All they needed was a bed.

Actually, all they probably needed was a floor.

Oh crap, and condoms—which she didn't have.

Maybe that was for the best. She wasn't going to follow the Spark guidelines for how far and how fast to go with a man, but she didn't need to go all the way before even making it to date number *one*.

The water running in the bathroom shut off and panic—exciting and pleasurable panic—gripped her. She lowered the dimmer and sat on her bed, heart in her throat, until she heard the bathroom door open. Footsteps, then silence, more footsteps and the kitchen went dark.

Footsteps, and Mercer was in the threshold in a T-shirt and boxers. He looked her in the eye. "This door get blown open?"

"No. I guess I left it open."

"Guess you did." And that was all anyone said for a little while.

She'd been afraid it would be awkward now, with intention behind whatever was coming, instead of those earlier mutual, spontaneous lapses in good sense. But it wasn't awkward. It was mindless and fast, wholly instinctual.

He was on her in seconds, pushing her onto her back, his weight feeling sinful against her hips as he braced himself above her. She welcomed his kiss, deep and aggressive and everything Mercer, as primal as a man ought to be. He lit her up like no one ever had, on a pure and animal level, a connection no measure of logic could predict.

He got his knees between hers and she swept her palms down his body, filled her lungs with the smell of his soap, felt the beads of water still clinging to his bare arms. Between her legs she could feel him, stiff and ready. Somewhere in the back of her mind, she had boundaries to establish. She commanded her mouth to find a purpose outside of tasting his, and tore her lips away.

"How far are we going?"

"Won't know till we get there."

"I haven't got any condoms." She gasped, unsure how she'd gone from lying on her back to being held to his chest, legs wrapped around his waist. He stood and carried her out of the room and past the kitchen.

"What are you doing?"

"Faster than bringing the condoms to you." He pushed the door to his dark room open with his shoulder and set her on his bed. It felt sexy, sitting there, smelling him everywhere in this private space. Still, Jenna wasn't sure how comfortable she actually wanted to get.

As he rooted through a dresser drawer, she said, "I wasn't upset about not having condoms."

He turned to her, streetlight glinting off the shiny plastic square in his hand. "Oh?"

"Give it to me."

He crossed to the bed and handed it over. Jenna tucked it beneath a pillow. "I'm in charge of when that thing gets used. *If* it gets used."

"The woman always is."

"Good."

"Where were we?"

In a breath they were on their sides, legs tangling, hands exploring. The kissing grew shallow and their breathing heavy. Everything about him was sexy. His wet hair, the firmness of his shoulders and his chest, the heat of his skin. Memories flashed through her head, of watching him in the gym not even an hour before. He could do extraordinary things to an opponent with that deadly body. What on earth could he do to *her?*

She sighed as Mercer cupped her breast and edged his body lower, kissing her collarbone as he fondled her. She shifted her legs, welcoming the taunting brush of his erection against her thigh. She tugged the front of his shirt up a few inches and stroked her palm over his bare, hard stomach, fingertips brushing his waistband and the soft hair hiding just behind it.

"Jenna."

There was a rasp to his voice, the same gruffness she imagined might possess him as he stepped into a ring. Damn, she was objectifying him again. But she'd never moved this fast with a guy before, and he was the perfect man—the perfect body—to be reckless with. Whatever they had, it was bigger than either of them.

Charged with lust, she tugged until he peeled his shirt away. With a coaxing push, he rolled onto his back. Jenna slung a leg over his waist to straddle him. She couldn't get close enough to this man.

He swore, hands flying to her hips to hold their bodies tight, center to center. She pulled her camisole up and off. They were bathed in yellowy streetlight, harsh and gritty and urban, just like the man beneath her. The honk of a car horn, the screech of brakes, the quarreling of strangers below on the sidewalk…bring it on. Whatever happened, she wanted the quintessential Boston experience, as brash and unapologetic as this fling.

Mercer's hands slid up her belly to her breasts, kneading as she undulated her hips, torturing them both with the friction through her damnable pajama bottoms.

"Let your hair down," he said.

She tugged the elastic from her ponytail.

"Jesus, you're sexy."

And you're extraordinary, she wanted to tell him, as she memorized every exceptional, intimidating contour of his bare body. She missed his hand wraps, even fantasized what those padded gym mats would feel like under her back… There she went again, with the fetish she hadn't even known she had.

"Take those frigging pants off, for the love of Christ." He tugged at the drawstring and she rolled to the side, both of them fighting to be the one to strip them away. No man had ever made her feel this *wanted* before, as if he couldn't control himself, nor had any man made her feel the same in return. A need this fierce and primal.

He climbed on top of her, shoved his knees beneath her thighs and ground their bodies together, just slightly too rough for comfort, just exactly perfect. His breaths became grunts, so like the noises she'd heard him make when he was working out. She scraped her nails down his side, angling her hips and welcoming the rough drag of his hard cock against her soft folds. He tilted his hips back, letting her feel the insistent press of his head between her legs, the thin barriers of cotton as maddening as a straightjacket.

"This is such a stupid idea," Mercer said, sounding happy about it.

"I know." She got lost staring at his torso, at the explicit flex of his chest and abs as he rubbed his erection against her. All this plus an even more enticing sight, if she chose to make use of that all-access pass she'd tucked beneath the pillow. With another man, she'd have said no, save it for the next date, savor the baby steps. But this might be—this *should* be—the only night she and Mercer made this mistake together. If she was going to binge, no point stopping at a slice; she'd eat the whole damn cake.

She pushed at his chest. "Get your shorts off."

She joined him, both of them sitting up and wrestling away their underwear. Then he was on her again, the hot press of his bare cock against her thigh tightening her like a spring.

"Mercer."

A groan answered her as he fumbled his hand between their bodies, centering his shaft along her lips. She was beyond ready, and with one, two, three strokes he was slick from her, their friction wet and dangerous and hotter than the best sex she'd ever had. He clasped her knees, gaze locked on the action happening between them. That fascinating face looked strained and fierce, lips parted. He was intriguing at rest, handsome when he smiled. But this…this was the only expression she ever wanted to see him wearing. Only one look could possibly thrill her more, and that would be the one he wore when he slid inside her.

She shoved her arm under the pillow, and the crinkle of the plastic snapped his attention to her hand.

She ripped open the condom and he took it from her, leaning back to roll it down his length. He was a bigger man than she'd had before, but the intimidation was fleeting. Before she could take a final, bracing breath, he was at her entrance. No asking, "Are you ready?" No caution. No resistance or protest from her body as he pushed inside, so deep their hips touched.

He swore again, and she dragged her nails down his ribs and sides. Even in the sickly ambient light she could see the red stripes that rose on his skin.

With a groan he braced his arms at her sides, thighs nudging hers wider, and began to thrust. She wrapped her legs around his waist, angled her hips to welcome him as deep as she could. She'd never felt this need before, this urgent craving to be possessed by someone. He was surely wrecking her for every slender, deferring academic who might come after, wrecking her entire perception of what her "type" was.

"You feel amazing." His eyes were shut, as though he wanted nothing distracting him from the sensation.

"So do you." He felt exactly as he should—big, rough, forceful. She watched his body owning hers, her pleasure mounting.

His eyes opened. "You need anything special? To get off?"

Not exactly poetry, but his words encapsulated what this was, a mutual itch-scratching, two animals taking what they wanted from each other.

"My clit."

Mercer leaned back on his haunches, slowing his thrusts, catching his breath. When it seemed the madness had left him, he put his palm to her mound, thumb on her clitoris. "Tell me how," he said, starting to rub.

"Lighter. And faster."

He followed her instructions perfectly, the rough pad of his thumb stroking her even better than she could do herself. And it went far beyond the touch—it was the sight of his body, the smell of him, the slap of his skin against hers. The least romantic, most frantic sex of her life. And it blew every slow, candlelit seduction clear out of the water.

He felt *right.* So right it scared her.

As she edged closer to release, she fantasized about how he would be when he neared the finish himself. Fast. Fast and vocal. Picturing it had her speeding toward orgasm, imagining his face, mean and needy. She swore as the first spasm struck, grasped his arm and neck and held on, riding the pleasure until it turned to pain, his thumb against her clit too much to take. She pulled his hand away, panting and dizzy.

"Jesus, Jenna." He surprised her then. He kept his hips still, dropping to his elbows to slide his hands beneath her back, kissing her neck and jaw as she caught her breath.

She cleared her throat. "You were right. You're even better at sex than you are at kissing."

He made a satisfied, happy noise against her throat, then rose on straight arms and looked her in the eyes.

She stroked his arms. "Your turn. What do you need?"

He laughed. "About eight seconds of your time, I suspect."

"What would you *like,* then?"

"To make you do some work."

"You're on."

He slid out and they switched positions, Mercer piling three pillows at the head of the bed so that as he lay down, he was only half-reclined. He put his hands to his hips. "C'mere."

She straddled him, welcoming his hard heat back inside her body. He couldn't ever be deep enough, close enough.

He brought his knees up, cradling her in his lap. Bracing her hands against the wall, she found her rhythm, thrilling at his grunts and groans and the way his eyes seemed to record everything she was doing. She paused as he unhooked her bra, then she slipped it off for him. As she began to move again, he put his hands to her breasts, not holding them, merely letting her nipples brush his palms with each roll of her hips. She could feel her excitement mounting all over again, from his touch, from the taunting friction of his base on her clit with each withdrawal. Raw brick beneath her palms. Raw, male breaths punctuating their sex.

"That's so good. I'm so close," he muttered.

So was Jenna. Her body craved the same motions his did, and as her second climax began to rise, his pleasure was reaching its own crescendo. He grasped her hips, issuing orders, forcing the speed and aggression he needed.

"Yeah." His teeth were gritted, eyes narrowed. His hips trembled beneath her, body begging. The look on his face excited her more than any physical sensation.

She came apart just as he neared the edge. He realized what was happening, the idea of it seeming to strike him like a whip. He swore. He held her hips still, thrusting up into her as he came, holding her hard.

When he let her go, she flopped to the mattress beside him. He left her only for a second to ditch the condom, and for minutes on end the room was filled with their heavy inhalations, occasionally accompanied by the odd voice from the street, the flare of an engine starting up, the slam of a car door.

You can't wake up next to him tomorrow. She had to get back to her own bed....

She blinked, realizing she'd nodded off. Better find her clothes and...

Again she jerked awake. Mercer's deep breathing said he'd succumbed to postsex male narcolepsy. Sounded awfully inviting. Still, she really ought to...

The thought abandoned her, and Jenna fell asleep, logical brain finally silent.

"Whoa."

Mercer woke early, surprised for a moment to find a woman beside him. And not just any woman.

The clock said it was five-forty and the room had gone chilly. He wanted to pull the covers over Jenna, but he couldn't free them without waking her. And waking her would probably rouse her from her orgasm-induced judgment lapse, and that would send her lovely, pale, naked body retreating to her own room. Tricky one.

Slow as tar, he crept from the bed, then padded to the living room and grabbed the old afghan from the back of the couch. He managed to drape it over her, but she roused as he climbed into bed beside her. *Damn.*

She made a soft noise of alarm.

He brushed the hair from her face. "Go back to sleep."

"What time is it?"

"Nearly six. You sure you didn't mean to ask, 'What the hell am I doing here?'"

"I know exactly what I'm doing here," she mumbled. "Arguing with you, which is no surprise." She yawned, then tucked herself tighter under the covers.

Pleased she hadn't bolted awake and out the door, Mercer relaxed, feeling warm from far more than the blanket.

Such a bad instinct, though. There was a semiuniversal rule observed by professional fighters—no sex in the three weeks preceding a match. Just stay away from women, period. They made you nuts, screwed with your focus, cooled your fire. All that pent-up testosterone was best saved and redirected to make yourself go berserk in the ring. Mercer hadn't had a paid fight of his own in three years, but he still thought it was a wise philosophy. He loved women in all kinds of capacities, but life *was* infinitely simpler when there wasn't one in the picture. Jenna complicated his life plenty with their clothes still on, and it was probably the worst romantic decision he'd ever made, waking up here naked with her. Though it hadn't felt like a decision. Felt like goddamn force of nature.

Just as Mercer was settling back down for another hour's sleep, reality intruded. Loudly. His phone buzzed on the side table, and when he saw Rich's number on the screen, it could only mean one thing. He hit Talk before the ringer could kick in, then left the room, closing the door behind him.

"Lemme guess—your crappy-ass car's broke down on the Tobin Bridge."

"No, I'm downstairs. I just forgot my gym keys."

Mercer rolled his eyes. "We've gotta get a keypad."

"C'mon, man. Bobby's down here. Don't make this OCD bastard late for his workout."

Mercer heard the man in question grumble something in the background.

"Fine. Lemme get some clothes on." He clicked the phone off and headed back to his room. Jenna was sitting up, afghan hugged to her chest.

"Sorry. Rich locked himself out. I have to go down and let him in."

She nodded through a yawn.

Mercer yanked boxers up his legs and grabbed a T-shirt. "Go back to sleep."

He jogged downstairs and glared at his friend a moment through the glass door, then flipped the bolt.

"Thanks, man." Rich swept in, giant Bobby and his gym bag right behind him, and Mercer led them down to the gym and unlocked the double doors.

Bobby was as OCD as Rich made out, and as soon as the lights were on he was heading for the warm-up area, clearly irked to be two minutes behind his daily regimen.

Rich gave Mercer and his outfit a glance. "Don't dress up on my account. But now you're awake, you wanna put some pants on and run drills with me?" He swiped a couple elbows in the air between them.

"Hell no. I'm going back to bed."

"Wow, grumpy. I interrupt something good?"

It was a joke, but Mercer flinched, a deadly tell to a fellow fighter.

Rich's face fell. "Oh shit. Sorry, man. I did, didn't I?"

"Never mind. I'll see you at ten with coffee."

"Coffee and all the horny details," Rich teased, but when Mercer didn't reply quick enough, Rich's expression shifted again, realization dawning. "Whoa. It's not Jenna, is it? Did you bone Jenna?"

Mercer caught Rich in the shin with a kick. "I didn't *bone* anybody."

"Did you make sweet, sensitive love to Jenna, though? Because that is *weird*. Monty's daughter… Basically your dad's daughter. That makes her, like, your stepsister, Merce."

"Shut up."

"He would *murder* you if he was alive."

"I'll murder you right now if you don't shut the hell up about it."

Rich put his hands up. "Fine. But it's wicked creepy, just so you know."

"See you later." Mercer jogged back up the stairs, annoyed. And was even more annoyed to hear the shower running when he got to the apartment.

Probably for the best. Maybe they'd been spared an awkward shared waking, or some quick tumble that would've only made things more confusing. He wouldn't have minded a peek at her naked body in the daylight, though.

An idea he'd been toying with resurfaced, and Mercer decided it was a good one. When Jenna emerged from the shower, towel wrapped around her trunk, he offered her a goofy smile. She returned it with something a bit cagier, a good-natured smirk.

"Morning," she said.

"Morning. Sorry about that. Not the most relaxing way to wake up."

She shrugged and Mercer wished he hadn't noticed the dots of water on her shoulders, or how goddamn sexy she looked with wet hair and eyelashes and no makeup.

"It's fine," she said. "Probably good that I'm up so early. I have a million things to do today."

"I'll bet. And actually, I'll make all that a little easier for you, and get out of your hair for the weekend."

"Oh?"

He nodded. "Delante could use a couple nights away from his family drama. I'm gonna drive him down to Hartford, have him spar with a couple guys a buddy of mine trains there. Get him focused. Plus it'll get me away from you, since my boy's not the only one around here who's losing their focus."

She blushed, and Mercer wondered if she thought he meant her, or himself. Both of them, probably. And it looked as though it'd take nothing less than crossing state lines to keep them apart.

"Not the worst idea," she agreed.

"Probably be back Sunday noontime. If I don't run into you before I head out, have a good weekend."

"You too. You want coffee? I'll start it once I'm dressed."

"Nah, I better get downstairs. Start figuring out how to get my shifts here covered on such short notice."

"Okay. Well, have a good trip, if I don't see you."

"I will."

With a nervous-looking smile, she headed for her room, closing the door softly. Mercer's breath had been high in his chest, and he let it out with a noisy sigh. Definitely for the best that he clear out for a couple nights. One look at her and he'd remember everything that had happened the night before, jump her and either get himself slapped or laid again, and he wasn't honestly sure which was preferable.

He headed down to the gym. The more steps he put between his body and Jenna's, the safer it was for everyone involved.

7

JENNA SPENT THE morning composing an ad to find her future assistant. Once it was uploaded to the best job-listings sites, she turned her energy to redecoration tasks.

At the sound of shouting, Jenna fumbled and the metal ribbon of her tape measure recoiled into its case and caught her thumb. "Ow."

She'd been measuring the front windows for blinds, and after a short silence more shouting drifted down the hall from the gym. Seconds later, Delante came stomping past. He caught sight of her on the other side of the glass, stopping to stare. His gaze was intense, unmistakably angry.

Jenna's heart pounded but she did her best to fake calm. "Everything okay?" she called.

The teenager looked down a moment, jaw flexing, then stepped to the doorway. "You own this place now, right?"

Panic gripped her. Had Mercer told his trainee she might have to close the gym? "Yeah, I do."

"So you're, like, Merce's boss?"

"Uh, technically. But—"

"Can you tell him to lay off me, then? Dude's driving me nuts. Busting my balls, like..." He trailed off, a violent inhalation seizing his massive shoulders. "Just tell him to quit riding me."

"I'm sure he's only pushing you as far he knows you're capable—"

"It's not that. Dude needs to chill. He makes it sound like this tournament's the only thing in the world. Like I don't got other shit to take care of."

She bit her lip. "Right… Would you like a cup of coffee or something?" She wasn't sure why she was offering, except she knew the kid needed to talk. And sure, she was technically the boss. Might as well do a good job, even if it was temporary. She owed guys like Delante that much.

He thought about it for a few breaths, then surprised her by saying, "Yeah, okay."

She waved him in and filled a mug from the French press she'd brought down.

"Thanks."

"Have a seat." She did the same, sitting in the chair behind the desk and wondering how often her father might have sat here, talking with kids like Delante. He filled the space with a potent mix of sweat and a dizzying choice of cologne. The smells that passed for manhood at nineteen. "So, Mercer's getting on your nerves?"

"Yeah. He's always riding my ass, like he's my dad or something. I told him I had to cut back on training, so I can get a job."

"And he told you you couldn't?"

"No, he was all like, 'Okay, we gotta change your schedule up, then, so you can do both.' And I was like, dude, I gotta sleep. This shit ain't my whole life. It's *his* whole life but, like, I got other responsibilities, you know?"

Jenna nodded. "Mercer cares a lot about you. And your potential—"

"I am *so sick* of that word."

"I'll bet. But he sees something in you. He sees a future for you in fighting. I'm sure he only wants you to succeed."

"Well, I gotta succeed way faster. He don't get that. He ain't gotta live my life when he leaves that stupid gym. I need money now, and he's like, 'Wait four weeks, until the match.' Dude, that's, like, *forever*. I can't wait till then. I got shit to take care of."

For the love of God, don't let it be a pregnancy.

"Now he's all like, 'Okay, pack some clothes, we're going to Connecticut.'"

"Might do you guys good to be stuck in a car for a few hours. He can't shout orders at you like down in the gym."

"Yeah, right."

"No, really. I know he's a taskmaster downstairs, but go along for the trip, then let him know he needs to back off on your schedule. He's a reasonable guy. I'm sure he'll understand if you just explain. Calmly."

Delante shook his head a moment, then cracked an unexpected smile, laughed softly. "You're such a chick."

She smiled back. "I know."

He looked around the office. "So you're opening some dating service, right?"

She nodded. "Like the personals sites do, only more...personal. Old-school."

"That's pretty cool, I guess."

Inspiration struck. "You said you need some fast money?"

"Hell yeah."

"Well, I'm going to be having this office and the apartment upstairs redone over the next couple months. I can probably get you some work helping—basic stuff like moving furniture, painting, sanding, maybe picking things up for me, if you've got a car. If you're interested..."

"If it's money, I'm interested. And I got a car."

"Okay. Good." Good for Delante, though possibly an invitation for yet more hassle and complication for Jenna. But if it kept the kid around the gym and out of the trouble Mercer had implied waited for him elsewhere, it seemed a smart gesture. Though she probably should have asked Mercer first.

"Give me your number and I'll let you know when I've got a job that needs doing." She pulled out her phone and opened a new contact.

He started to tell her the digits, then paused. "Your dad wouldn't probably want me doing that stuff for money. He'd probably have said I should do it for free."

"Well, I'm not my father. And it's hard work, and hard work deserves payment. Plus I'd probably get scammed for a lot more by a moving company or a contractor, so you're still doing me a favor."

He submitted and gave her his number.

She saved the entry. "Great. And you'll go with Mercer tonight, to Hartford? And tell him how you're feeling? Oh gosh, you're right. I do sound like a chick."

He laughed. "Yeah. I can't believe you're Monty's daughter. But sure, I'll go. Only 'cause now I don't have to spend the weekend hustling for work. So, thanks."

"You're welcome. Good luck."

When Delante left, Jenna felt proud in a way she hadn't in weeks—the same happy feeling she got when two people she introduced at a cruise mixer wound up making out in a dark corner of the ship's ballroom. Solving problems felt nice, romantic or otherwise.

She was just settling down with some paperwork when another visitor appeared in the door—Rich.

She smiled to cover up the weird little tug of intimidation he triggered. "Hello."

He smiled back, his black eye off-putting. "Hey. Mind if I interrupt?"

She wheeled her chair back from the desk and slapped

her laptop closed. "Go for it. Any excuse to put off tackling these forms."

He turned a chair around, straddling it. He had the weirdest vibe—intensely, *electrically* relaxed. He fixed her with his dark eyes and grinned.

"Yes?"

"So, I know you and Merce have been... You know."

She frowned.

"Don't freak—he didn't tell me. I just knew, since the only thing that'd make him turn down a chance to scrap is a naked woman in his bed. And since you're sleeping up there already..."

She sighed. "Yes, fine. Well deduced. Have you come to gossip?"

"Just came to find out what your intentions are with my friend."

She laughed. "Seriously? That's awfully proper of you."

"They don't call me the Prince just because of this beautiful mug." He pointed to his face and flashed her a smug—and indeed princely—smile. "Anyhow, yeah, I'm mostly here to confirm the scandal. And to make sure you know that Mercer's pretty much a commitmentphobe."

"Yes, he mentioned that." Though for irrational reasons, it stung to have the fact corroborated. "You don't have to protect my feelings, though it's sweet...sort of. And very nosy."

"I know. But you're Monty's daughter, and he was my mentor for, like, fifteen years, so that makes you my honorary cousin or something. And I'd tell my cousin if she was getting mixed up with a guy that's going to break her heart, even if the guy was basically her stepbrother, since your dad was like Mercer's—"

"Yes, I follow. Thank you. Don't worry, though. I'm a matchmaker. I know all about spotting men who aren't relationship material, remember?"

"Sure. Of course. Just being a good cousin."

She thought the conversation was over, but Rich dawdled, drumming his fingers along the back of the chair, not meeting her gaze.

"Was there something else?"

"So… When's the matchmaking business actually opening?"

"I'll start collecting new clients as soon as all the property stuff is squared away, in the next couple weeks. But I'm not officially open until mid-September, when I'm throwing a mixer. Why?"

"What's it cost?"

She blinkcd at him. "You want to join?"

"Sure, why not?"

Why not indeed? Rich was undeniably handsome. Accomplished, if in an unusual field, and he'd traveled. But for the female clients she'd be catering to…

"I'm not sure I'm the best service for you. The women I'm going to be matching—I doubt they'd be your type."

"I haven't got a type, aside from 'conscious female.' You mean I'm not *their* type, right?"

"Well…"

He smirked, clearly annoyed. "Not sure what else you need in a guy—I'm single, I'm charming, I made nearly a hundred grand last year in prize money…"

She blinked. Damn, Rich ought to buy the gym himself. "That *is* quite impressive."

"Spent it all paying for my mom's heart surgery, but the first part looks good on paper. Plus you must need photos for the profiles, right?" Another flash of that deadly grin, and Rich framed his face with his hands. It wasn't a bad point. A face like that *would* look nice on the home page—once his eye healed.

"Yes, well. I won't turn anyone away unless they've got

a serious criminal record or attitude problem, so you're welcome to apply."

"Excellent. Well, I'll quit bugging you." He stood and swiveled the chair back the way it should be. "I'll see you around, cousin."

Impulse struck. "Rich, wait."

He turned back, studying her. "You okay?"

"I'm not sure."

"Oh God, you're in love with Mercer."

It was so unexpected, she laughed and shook her head. "Could you close the door, please?"

His shapely black brows rose. "You in love with *me?* Miss Wilinski, we're cousins."

She shot him a pointed look and he relented, shutting the door.

"Have a seat." When he did, she took a deep breath. "You were really close to my father, right?"

"Yeah. He was like my second dad. I used to joke with him that he made me a quarter Polish. Can't say I knew him the way Mercer did, but yeah. We were real close."

"Do you think…? Do you believe he was innocent of all that criminal stuff?"

"I was about seventeen when that shit was going down. I was clueless about anything aside from who I got to punch next."

"I don't mean, do you *know* for sure if he was really involved. I mean, do you *feel* he was? Was he capable of that?"

Rich looked thoughtful. "I want to say no, he'd never do that. But your dad was a complicated guy. I think he had his secrets. Every couple months, he'd disappear for a day or two. He'd tell us ahead of time, but he never said where he was going. I want to say I knew the guy, but I can't. Not enough to say if my wanting to believe he was innocent is intuition, or loyalty."

She frowned. "Well, thanks for your honesty."

"Is it killing you, not knowing for sure?"

"A little." When he'd been nothing more than a stranger to her, she'd believed the worst with no qualms. Now that she'd connected with a man he'd nearly raised, a *good* man... Suddenly she wanted him to be worthy of all the faith Mercer had put in him.

"If you want my advice," Rich said, standing, "let yourself believe the best. That's what the rest of us do."

She nodded, not much comforted. "I'll try. See you later."

From the doorway Rich called, "You watch yourself with Mercer."

"For whose benefit?" she called back, but he'd already gone.

JENNA DIDN'T CROSS PATHS with Mercer for the rest of the morning, though he could have passed by the office any number of times. She'd kept her eyes glued to her screen, filling out a million online forms for the franchise and window-shopping for furniture to turn the front entryway into a welcoming waiting area. She was nervous to spot him, frankly, now that she had no clue what to make of him.

Damn it, why did he have to be so good in bed? She'd never understood why some of her friends stayed with crappy boyfriends for longer than they should, claiming, "But the sex is *insane.*"

Okay, fine. She got it now. And Mercer was far from a crappy boyfriend. He was funny and levelheaded and passionate, and pretty wonderful. He was also far from being her boyfriend. A fact that made her sadder than it ought to.

It wasn't until three, when her eyes were glazed and her stomach was growling from a lack of lunch, that she saw him again. She looked up as he knocked on the doorframe.

"Hey. Come in." Talking to him from his old chair—her

dad's old chair—felt too weird, so she stood and skirted the desk.

Mercer had a gym bag slung over his shoulder and car keys in his hand. "Thought I'd say 'bye before I head out, make sure you don't need anything, roommate-wise."

"Nope, I'm good."

"And Rich should have everything under control downstairs. Got my number, just in case?"

"I do. Did you talk to Delante?"

"Yeah, and he said he talked to you. I was afraid I'd have to go on some reconnaissance trip to Mattapan after he stormed out, but whatever you said to him, he's way calmer, so thanks."

"Don't thank me quite yet."

"No?"

She chewed her lip. "I'm not sure. He said he needed money, so I told him I'd give him some work moving furniture for me over the next couple weeks."

"Okay, great."

"Yeah?"

"Sure. Why wouldn't I be happy with that? Whatever keeps him close is fine by me. More than fine."

Jenna relaxed. "That's what I hoped. But I was worried I might be stepping on your toes. Or maybe you didn't want him working at all, or I was going to risk putting his back out or something."

"The kid's a tank—I do worse damage to him before nine a.m. than lifting a love seat ever could. I'd rather he not work at all, but that's not realistic. So it's a perfect compromise, really."

"Great. Well, enjoy your trip."

"I will now, thanks to you. If I'm lucky, after a few hours on the road I can knock all this nonsense about money out of his head."

"I hope it's not anything really serious, like a preg—"

Mercer cut her off with a loud shushing noise, clamping his hands over his ears. "Don't even get me worrying about that kind of stuff or I'll wake up with a headful of white hair."

She nodded and made a zipping motion across her lips.

"It's not that, anyhow. His little sister's starting college next month, and he's stressed about the price tag. Trying to be the man of the house. But if he wins this match and gets signed, he can pay her next four years' tuition with five rounds' worth of work. He's just spooked. It's the fight of his life next month."

"No pressure."

"Exactly."

"When you get back…could you tell me more about my dad?"

He blinked, clearly surprised. "Yeah, I'd be happy to. You trying to make peace in your head?"

"I have this feeling I missed out, only getting my mom's perspective."

"You're always welcome to mine."

If only her dad had offered her *his,* but that was a useless thing to wish for.

"Speaking of your dad, I left you something on your bed."

"What?"

"You'll see. Have a good weekend."

"Drive safe."

He began to turn then stopped. "And Jenna?"

She raised her eyebrows, then Mercer's mouth stole her gasp, his kiss firm and brief. Jenna's pulse raced. He smiled wickedly as he broke away, and she scanned the hall for witnesses.

"Thanks again," he said. "Now, get the hell out of my head."

She faked offense, secretly aglow at the gesture. "Only if you get out of my office."

A final grin and he left. What a perplexing, annoying man. She called it a day at five and gathered her coffee press and computer and locked the office. She waved to a now-familiar face on her way to the back stairs, one of the many guys who'd stopped by to share their condolences. Funny how a few days ago these men had made her so nervous, but now that she'd spoken to them, knew some of their names, they went beyond intimidating bodies and damaged faces to regular old people. People who could bench press her, but people all the same.

She dumped her things on the counter and headed for her room to change into comfier clothes. She'd forgotten Mercer's parting words, and was surprised by the plastic storage tub sitting on her bed. As she snapped each latch open, she tried and failed to guess what it could be.

Inside the box were more boxes—shoeboxes mostly, and a cigar box on top with *Jenna* scrawled on it. She flipped it open and sucked in a breath, staring at a photo of herself in her sixth-grade band uniform. She pulled out the stack and flipped through it. Her first day of camp. Waving a sparkler around on the Fourth of July, swimming in her grandparents' pool.

When she'd seen them all, she turned them over, surprised again. Each had a note from her grandma—her mom's mother—written on it in her distinctive cursive, dating and detailing the event. Tears welled. Her grandma had passed away just two years before, and this was so like her…dismissing the drama and doing what she felt was right. And her dad had cared enough to keep them.

Setting the cigar box aside, she pulled out a shoebox next. More photos, and a couple of videotapes labeled *Jenna's First Meet* and *Family Reunion '02*. She wondered if he'd watched these, and what he'd done as he did. Drink? Cry? Strain to feel anything for the girl on the screen, by then a stranger to him?

A third box also held photos and tapes, but the one on the bottom, the biggest of the stack, didn't.

It held letters, bound together by the dozen with rubber bands. From her grandmother, she imagined…but no. That wasn't her grandmother's writing. And the return address was *here,* the apartment she was sitting in, and the letters were addressed to Jenna, at her parents' place in Sacramento, where she'd grown up. She frowned.

Why would her father write her letters, and never send them? Why bother with an envelope? Why bother with *stamps?* Then she realized, those stamps had all been processed. These letters and cards had all reached the house, but they must have been collected and shipped back, probably with a bitter note from Jenna's mom to quit sending them, that Jenna didn't want these.

She noticed her hands shaking, and couldn't tell if it was from nerves or shock or anger.

She remembered the few times she'd spoken to her dad on the phone, and realized she couldn't recall ever having been summoned for the call. No, she must have answered the phone herself with no one around to play bouncer. Her dad's voice had sounded strange…off. She'd mentioned that to her mother once, and been told he was probably drunk. She wondered now if maybe he'd been crying, relieved to have reached her.

She chose one card to slit open. It was a lumpy pink envelope the post office had stamped nearly twenty-five years earlier, a week before her fifth birthday. She slid out a girlie card with a hula-hooping cat on the cover, shedding ancient glitter across her bedspread. A bracelet fell out. Plain silver links with a lobster-claw clasp, one tiny silver charm attached, shaped like a star. She opened the card.

Happy birthday, pumpkin!
Miss you so much. Wish I could give you your birthday hugs in person. Hope you like your present. Your aunt helped me pick it out, and she said you should add a new charm to it every year. But don't wear it yet—it's too big and you might lose it.

Be good for your mom. Hope I'll see you at Christmas.
Love, Dad

Jenna felt odd. Drunk without a sip of alcohol.

She tore the rubber bands from the other stacks and squeezed them all until she'd amassed a pile with lumps in them. Most had been sent around Christmas and birthdays, a couple on Valentine's Day, and each held a charm. A clarinet, from the time she'd first started playing. A little pair of swim goggles and a tiny whistle after she'd gotten her first camp counselor job. More generic ones as well, hearts and birds and music notes, a shamrock on St. Patrick's Day. There had to be twenty of them, at least. And after the first stack of letters came back, then the next and the next, he'd kept sending them.

Jenna glanced around the room, feeling scared and alone. She wished Mercer were around, so she could demand some answers. Why had her father continued to send her letters and cards when he knew they'd never get to her? And why on earth hadn't he sent them to her grandmother, who'd maybe have seen fit to sneak them into Jenna's hands?

She tried to picture him, big scarred hands fumbling through a rack of charms at a jewelry store, but she could barely remember.

She pulled on a sweater and slipped her feet into flip-flops and headed downstairs. The gym was busy, men getting in their evening workouts. Jenna was ignored as she wandered to the back wall.

Normally she'd have paused at the clippings about Mercer, but she skimmed the articles, stopping only when she caught glimpses of her dad. Usually in someone's corner, hand on some tired boxer's shoulder. A big man, heavy in his middle age, with a mustache and thick head of hair, wire-framed glasses. He looked very...real. Very human, and very happy in

OFFICIAL OPINION POLL

Dear Reader,

Since you are a book enthusiast, we would like to know what you think.

Inside you will find a short Opinion Poll. Please participate in our poll by sharing your opinion on 3 subjects that are very important to all of us.

To thank you for your participation, we would like to send you **2 FREE BOOKS** and **2 FREE GIFTS!**

Please enjoy them with our compliments.

Sincerely,

Pam Powers

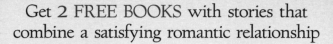

YOUR OPINION POLL
THANK-YOU FREE GIFTS INCLUDE:

▶ **2 HARLEQUIN® BLAZE™ BOOKS**
▶ **2 LOVELY SURPRISE GIFTS**

OFFICIAL OPINION POLL

YOUR OPINION COUNTS!
Please check TRUE or FALSE below to express your opinion about the following statements:

Q1 Do you believe in "true love"?

"TRUE LOVE HAPPENS ONLY ONCE IN A LIFETIME."
○ TRUE
○ FALSE

Q2 Do you think marriage has any value in today's world?

"YOU CAN BE TOTALLY COMMITTED TO SOMEONE WITHOUT BEING MARRIED."
○ TRUE
○ FALSE

Q3 What kind of books do you enjoy?

"A GREAT NOVEL MUST HAVE A HAPPY ENDING."
○ TRUE
○ FALSE

YES! I have placed my sticker in the space provided below. Please send me the **2 FREE books** and **2 FREE gifts** for which I qualify. I understand that I am under no obligation to purchase anything further, as explained on the back of this card.

151/351 HDL FVNU

FIRST NAME | LAST NAME

ADDRESS

APT.# | CITY

STATE/PROV. | ZIP/POSTAL CODE

HB-TF-03/13
Printed in the U.S.A.
© 2012 HARLEQUIN ENTERPRISES LIMITED.

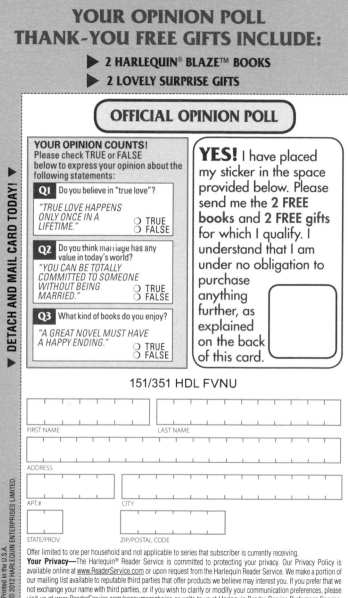

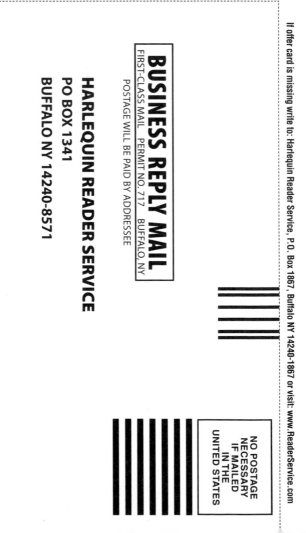

the shots where he wasn't shouting from the ropes. He looked loved, by the family he'd been so dedicated to.

Her throat tight and aching, Jenna escaped back upstairs. She poured herself a large glass of wine, and though it felt like an invitation to more confusion, sat down on her bed and opened the next envelope.

BY ELEVEN O'CLOCK, Jenna was a bit tipsy, and dehydrated from crying. She set the latest letter aside. There were still stacks and boxes to go, but she couldn't take any more.

She felt a thousand things. Heartsick for the man who'd sat down and written all those letters, trying to connect with a daughter who'd only grown more distant with each passing birthday and holiday. Angry with her mother. *Livid* with her mother. Above all, confused about her own feelings and doubting a lifetime's worth of assumptions she'd made about the man she'd so long ago quit calling her dad.

She considered phoning her mother and having it out, but she was too upset. Instead she opened her computer and searched her email for another number, dialing with shaky fingers. The line picked up after a couple tones.

"Yuh?"

"Mercer?"

"Hey, Jenna. Everything okay?" She heard sleep in his croaky voice.

"Everything's…weird." Her own voice was weak, too, tight with tears.

"Why, what's happened?"

"Nothing to get panicked about. But you know that big tub of stuff you left me?"

"Sure."

"Did you know there's letters in there?"

"No. I thought it was all photos and tapes. What kind of letters?"

"From my dad, to me. I've never seen them before."

She heard a grunt, the sound of him sitting up, she thought. "Are you okay?" he asked.

"I don't know. He sent them, dozens of them, and it looks like my parents must have returned them all. But he kept sending new ones.... It's weird. It's like he didn't realize I never got them, or..." She trailed off, overwhelmed.

"You sound upset."

"I am, a bit. A lot."

"Well, maybe he didn't really write those for you. After the first ones got returned, I mean. Maybe he wrote them for himself. To feel better about never talking to you or something, to feel like he was at least trying? It's hard for me to guess. He never told me about any letters."

"Right."

"Sorry, I wish I had more answers for you. And sorry if it messed you up, my leaving all that stuff on your bed. I thought it might be nice for you to go through the photos, with me away..."

"No, *I'm* sorry. For waking you up."

"No worries—it's not even midnight. Plus our motel's next to the freeway. If it wasn't you it'd be another sixteen wheeler going by five minutes from now." He yawned and Jenna wished she was there, that she could wrap herself around him and feel anchored to someone so strong and calm.

"I'll let you go, get back to sleep."

"You sure you're okay?"

"I will be. I was just...blindsided. I'm sorry I called you."

"Shut up about that. I'm glad you called. I'm glad I heard my phone and you got to talk to somebody."

"I am too."

"You gonna be okay?"

"Yeah." She nodded, reminding herself it was true—she *would* be okay. "I probably just need to sleep it off, wake up with a clear head. I drank a couple glasses of wine, which probably didn't help things much."

A soft laugh. "Probably not."

"Anyhow, thanks. I guess I'll see you Sunday. Have a good trip. Promise I won't interrupt you again."

"Jenna, I invite people to try to punch me in the face on a daily basis. I can handle getting drunk-dialed at eleven p.m."

Her cheeks warmed. "I'm not drunk."

"Maybe not, but you're cute when you've had a couple of glasses. Get some sleep, okay?"

She sighed, finally feeling more exhausted than upset. "I will. You too."

"'Bye now."

"'Bye."

She tossed her phone on the pillow and rubbed her throbbing temples, willing her racing brain to slow. The bedspread was covered in photos and envelopes, but her body felt leaden at the thought of gathering and reorganizing them.

An idea came, a bad one. Before she could change her mind, Jenna had brushed her teeth and washed her face, downed a couple of aspirin and tiptoed to Mercer's dark room. She crawled under his rumpled covers and breathed him in, swaddled herself in a facsimile of his warmth and strength. Hugging a pillow tight, she admonished herself for being this pitiful. Still, when she drifted off, she dreamed only of Mercer.

8

Thank goodness for Hartford.

The two-hour drive down had given Mercer and Delante a chance to breathe the same air without shouting at each other. When they got into town, Mercer had been in luck. One of his friend Dave's hottest kickboxing prospects was on hand and ready for a friendly spar with Boston's finest.

Life had started to feel elemental again, his responsibilities reduced to the task of keeping Delante on track…at least for a weekend. Then Jenna's call had come, reminding him that what he was feeling outside the ring was far from simple.

After they said goodbye he sat up in bed, watching the headlights streaming by, restless to the marrow. Knowing Jenna was back in Boston in a still-unfamiliar apartment, her dad's apartment—struggling to make sense of what she'd learned… If only he hadn't left her that box the one time he wasn't going to be around to run damage control.

Midnight came and went and Mercer gave up on sleep. He tried channel surfing in an attempt to bore himself into unconsciousness, but when one o'clock arrived and he'd failed to register a single thing that'd flashed by on the screen, he turned the TV off. Turned his light on. He dressed and pocketed his keys and scribbled a note to slide under Delante's door. Then he climbed into his car to start the long drive back to Boston.

JENNA'S EYES FLEW OPEN at the flip of a dead bolt.

She clutched Mercer's blanket to her chin, frozen. She glanced at the clock, wondering who on earth would show up at three-thirty. An ex of his? A friend? A burglar with superior lock-picking skills? A light came on past the hall—the living room. She shot upright, hugging the covers tighter.

"Who's there?" she shouted.

"It's just me."

Her heart attack ceased at the sound of Mercer's voice, then her worries flip-flopped, humiliation taking the place of fear.

More footsteps, then he called, "Jeez, where are you?"

"I'm, um, in your room." *In your bed, under your covers. Like a moron.*

He appeared in the doorway and eased the dimmer switch up. "What are you doing in here?"

Making a fool of myself. "I got overwhelmed after going through all the photos and cards in my own room. My dad's room, you know?" *Good save.*

"Oh, right."

"Sorry. That's probably a little creepy of me."

"Not really. Not like you haven't slept in that bed before." She smirked. "True."

He took a seat at the foot of his bed, laying a hand on her shin through the covers.

"What are you doing back?" she asked.

"I was worried about you."

She blinked. "Worried enough to drive all the way here in the dead of night?"

"Looks that way."

"Oh. Wow. And thank you. I feel bad now, dragging you away. I was upset—not, like, in danger or anything."

He shrugged. "You didn't drag me. Plus Delante'll be happy for a chance to sleep in, and I'll head back early. I won't miss anything aside from a bit of rest. Looks like you managed to nod off, at least."

"Yeah. Just not in my own room." She rolled her eyes to admit she realized how silly she was being.

"They're all your rooms."

The thought stung, reminding her he might not be here much longer. And he'd be gone because of her intrusion, same as the gym, come January. The thought saddened her. Could the place have actually *grown* on her, so soon? Possibly. And like it or not, she was falling for Mercer.

She sighed. "I should really give you your bed back."

"Move over," he said softly.

She slid to the side and he lay down beside her on top of the covers, clasping his fingers over his ribs.

You really like him, a thought whispered. *More than you've liked anybody before. And so, so fast.* "It was awfully nice of you, caring enough to come all the way back here."

"Well, I feel sort of responsible for you, with your dad gone. Not like your guardian or anything—nothing patronizing."

"Of course not."

"Just like… The same way I'm happy to watch over the gym for him." He turned to look at her, eyes full of kindness.

"I don't know what to make of him anymore." Him or this man he'd mentored.

"You still think he was involved in that shady shit that went down all those years ago?"

"I have no clue. But I grew up assuming he really didn't care about me, and now I know he did and I feel…just awful. It would've meant so much to him, my sending *him* a letter, a Father's Day card, and I never did. And I don't understand, either. He could have mailed all those letters to my grandma, and she'd have gotten them to me, behind my mom's back."

"You know," Mercer said, "your dad used to say the smartest thing your mom ever did was leave his ass and get you away from here. He didn't make any bones about the fact that he was a pretty lousy husband—unreliable and hot-headed—and that he regretted it."

Jenna held her tongue, lost for words.

"I was thinking about this the whole drive from Hartford. I think maybe he sent those letters and things where he did, knowing she'd have a chance to vet them. To show her he respected her wishes enough to let her have the final say in what was best for you."

"Maybe."

"It's just a guess. For all his shortcomings, your dad had a really strict code of ethics when it came to respect."

"It's as good a guess as any. Maybe I'll find more answers, the more I keep reading." A daunting thought. She sighed again, blinking up at the ceiling. "I feel like a jerk, that I showed up here just assuming I'd close the gym. I was so ready to side with my mom, and the franchise, and all the other business owners on the block, in condemning this place. Like, figuratively and pretty much literally."

"Yeah. We're the mangiest of underdogs."

"And I was ready to just lump you and all the other guys down there in some folder labeled 'stuff my dad cared about more than me.'"

"Does that mean…? What does that mean?"

"It means I'm softening. It means I'd like the gym to stay open, if we figure out a way to make it viable."

Mercer spoke quietly, as if physically holding back whatever hope he felt. "Would you extend the trial period?"

"I will. For as long as it takes to see any effects from the tournament. And I'll do my best to fund your improvements… the modest ones, at least. Enough to give it a real chance."

Mercer didn't say a word at first, just brought his lips to

her throat, kissing her softly and holding her tight. After a minute's quiet he rolled onto his back and murmured, "Thank you."

"You're welcome. I can't claim to know my dad yet, but it's what he would've wanted."

She sensed Mercer nodding in her periphery. They were silent for a few minutes, until a random thought drew a laugh from her lips.

"What?"

She turned onto her side. "Rich wants to join Spark."

"No surprise there. He's a shameless attention-whore. Bodes well for his fighting career, at least."

"Guess I won't be signing *you* up anytime soon," she teased.

"I like to think I do all right on my own." A funny little smile quirked his lips. "In fact, I recall doing better than just all right, not too long ago. Right in this bed."

She blushed, then let impulse guide her hand out from the covers to rest on his stomach. "You were right about all this being really confusing. About you and I being too many things to each other."

"For now, yeah. But before you know it, 'roommates' will be off that list."

She stroked his belly, barely realizing she was doing it until he covered it with his warm, rough palm.

"I got no clue what to do with you," he murmured.

"Ditto."

"Or any clue what to do with all these…feelings. About protecting you, or just frigging *caring* this much, you know?"

"Do you resent me a little, that my dad left this place to me instead of you?"

"Of course not. I've never been taught to think anybody owes me anything."

She nodded.

"And I don't share your priorities, but I can imagine that matchmaking means as much to you as fighting does to me. And I get that my life must seem just as weird to you as meddling in other people's romantic lives does to me. You want to help people fall in love. I want to help guys get real good at beating each other senseless. Neither of us is exactly aiming to save third-world orphans. We're just passionate about things. And nobody gets to choose what they're passionate about. It just chooses you."

"Again, levelheaded."

Another shrug. "I got a deep-rooted sense of fairness."

"That you do. I'm so glad it hasn't been punched out of you, yet." She sighed. "I really ought to give you your bed back so you can get a few hours' rest before you have to get back on the road."

He gave her hand a squeeze. "It was big enough for two last night."

Her face warmed, but not as deeply as her heart. "True."

"I've given up wanting us to make sense, Jenna. I'm useless at navigating any kind of human interaction more complicated than 'hit that guy before he hits you.'"

She smiled. "Come here."

He turned onto his side, and the kiss was soft and sweet, lazy. Normally she'd have been beyond hesitant to let a boyfriend of less than six months see her this way, all blotchy from crying, no makeup, hair a tangle, but there was no etiquette with Mercer, no games, none of her precious logic. He'd seen her businesslike, seen her wild and impulsive. He'd taken her spooked, late-night phone call and driven all the way back here to catch her sleeping in his bed. If he took her again, he'd get her as she was, messy and unsure.

She welcomed his tongue when he took the kiss deeper, his growing aggression feeling like a relief—a release.

"Take me," she murmured.

"You sure?"

"I am."

He left her just long enough to go to his dresser drawer, then set a condom on the side table. Jenna slept in a tee and shorts, and as Mercer climbed under the covers with her, the brush of his jeans against her bare legs felt all the more exciting. He climbed on top of her, chest warm against her breasts, and they kissed for an exquisite eternity, five minutes or ten or an hour—forever wouldn't have been long enough. This connection felt so right, so grounding and simple in its core, yet pulsing with such passion.

They shed their clothes slowly and in silence, layers shunted to a tangle at their feet. She sucked in her breath as his cock glanced her belly—warm, hard flesh, soft skin. She studied his back and hips with slow caresses, excited to have him in the light this time. She pushed the covers from him, and for a long minute they admired one another's bodies, his face looking as curious and fearless as she felt herself.

She tugged at his hips.

"Ready?"

"Yes."

He leaned back for the condom and slid it down his erection, then brought his chest back to hers. As she wrapped her legs around his waist, he entered her with a familiarity she'd never known with any other lover, as though their two bodies were designed exactly for this purpose, no other match possible.

"Tell me what you need," he whispered, setting a slow, steady rhythm.

She needed nothing more than this. No orgasm even, just proof that something in her life could feel this instinctual, beyond questioning or rationalizing. "Just this."

The deep, smooth slide of his cock hypnotized her, the soft tempo of his grunts and moans drawing her into him. She stroked his strong back, reveling in the flex of muscle, feeling like a part of a greater whole with this amazing man. He must have been feeling something beyond mere awe, however, and before long, his body's demands grew harsher. She let her hips tell him she was game for whatever he needed, mirroring his quickening thrusts, welcoming him deep.

"I'm close," he moaned.

"Take whatever you want." She held his head as he drove into her harder, faster. Coordination abandoned him and he sped frantically to release.

"Jenna—" Her name died in his throat as his hips pinned her, hard. She clawed his shoulder without meaning to, overcome by the animal urges he roused.

"God. Jenna." With a huff he rolled from her, stripping the condom. She was poised to cuddle, but he didn't give her the chance. In seconds he was edging down the bed, kicking the covers and their clothes to the floor, settling on his elbows between her thighs.

"I don't need anything," she reminded him softly, stroking his hair. The sex was wonderful, but it was the closeness she wanted. The security of simply having him near. Of knowing he'd driven all those miles to be with her.

He broke his gaze from her sex to meet her eyes. "You saying you don't want me to?"

"No…I'm not saying that, either."

A grin. "Good."

Jenna's priorities shifted the second his tongue touched her. The firm, slick caress traced the seam of her lips, and she wanted exactly what he was offering. Pleasure, equity. She let him coax her legs wider, invited his tongue deeper. He tasted and teased her for ages, then finally slid his talented, hungry mouth to her clit, the contact hot and violent as a lightning strike.

"Mercer." She raked her nails down his scalp.

In her head she replayed the visual of him taking her just minutes before. This strong, fearless man coming apart at the seams. She remembered how he'd been the last time they'd made love, beneath her, eyes recording her movements. Nothing in any logical questionnaire could ever have brought them together, but now she worried that if this didn't last, she might never find the same connection with anyone, ever again.

His soft grunts drew her out of the sad thoughts and back into the pleasure he was giving her. He slid two fingers inside, making her miss his cock with a startling ferocity.

"Mercer?"

He freed his mouth and met her gaze. "Yeah?"

"Is there any chance you've got a round two in you?"

"No guarantees, but we can find out." He left her to fetch a fresh condom and climbed back into bed beside her. He slid a hand to his cock, stroking himself.

"Not that what you were doing wasn't wonderful," she said. "It was just so wonderful it made me want more."

"You're dangerously good for my ego."

She watched his hand, saw him growing hard for her again. "Here," she said, reaching out.

He let her take over and she reveled in his response to her touch.

They kissed as she stroked him, then she felt his hand at her thigh, coaxing it wider. They broke apart, and when he grabbed the condom she took it from him, rolling it down his length. He slid his thigh between hers, holding her hip as he pushed inside. Forehead to forehead, they found their pace and angles. He reached between their bodies to tease her clit, making her gasp. Her palm stroked his backside and she admired the flex there as he took her deeply.

"You feel so good," she muttered.

He kissed her in perfect rhythm with their undulating bodies. When she came it was from everything, equally—his mouth and cock and fingers, from the comfort of his proximity and strength. As she fell back to earth, he rolled her onto her back and got both knees between hers, thrusting fast and frantic for half a minute before he groaned, back arching into his own release. With a disbelieving noise, he flopped onto his back next to her. She rolled to her side and laid her cheek against his shoulder.

"Wow," he said, wide eyes aimed at the ceiling. "I didn't know I was capable of that. Not since I was about twenty."

"A good coach will always push you beyond your limits," she teased, patting his chest.

"This going to be a regular thing, you ambushing me in my bed? Because I'll be honest, it's not exactly motivating me to move out any quicker."

She laughed. "I'm not feeling especially eager to see you go, myself."

He closed his hand around hers.

After a long silence she asked, "What will you tell Delante, about where you disappeared to?"

"I'll tell him the truth—I had to come home to tend to an emergency."

"I wouldn't exactly classify my emotional breakdown as an *emergency*."

"It was enough to bring me back, wasn't it?"

An unsettling sensation filled Jenna. She found the courage to ask him, point-blank, "What exactly do you feel for me?"

"Hell if I know."

"No, really. I don't want to sound clingy, but if this keeps happening, I *am* one of those girls who gets attached. I know this is all just for now, for however long it lasts. But if I found out in a week that you hooked up with another girl…I won't lie. It'd hurt. I'm wondering where we stand, I guess."

"Where we stand is that we're lying in my bed together," Mercer said. "I don't know exactly what you think my love life's about, but this doesn't happen to me that often. And if it does, there's almost always at least been a *date* involved. Really, you're the most casual fling I've had in ages."

"Oh."

"So if you're worried I might wind up doing something with some other woman next week, it's not going to happen. Nothing good ever came of multitasking, sex- or romance-wise."

"True." Still, she wished he'd say something more…reassuring. Something more personal, to let her know she had more than mere *dibs* on him. That maybe she had just a *little* piece of his heart.

"Plus I've never…" He trailed off with a sigh.

"Never what?" *Tell me tell me tell me.*

"Whatever we are…I've never been this bent out of shape over a woman before. I can't tell you if it's the sex or if it's the bad-idea factor, or what. But seriously, you've got me all screwed up in the head. A busload of naked women could unload at the curb and I doubt I'd notice. You're in here," he said, tapping his temple. "Like a splinter or something."

Jenna would have preferred if he'd tapped his chest, but she'd take whatever he gave. She relaxed against his shoulder. "I promise I'm not gunning to be your girlfriend or anything."

"You're just into commitment, even with your flings." He smoothed her hair back, voice dropping to a near-whisper. "Wouldn't run screaming if you were, though. Gunning to be my girlfriend, I mean."

Thump, thump, thump from her heart. "Really?"

"Nope."

"Oh."

He smirked. "Though I'd question your taste."

She laughed.

"But we can keep it simple. Just know that my bed and my body are yours to do with as you see fit."

She smiled. He was, without a doubt, the most reasonable man she'd ever met.

But another thought was still hovering, regarding another man who'd called this place home. Who'd called himself her father, when she'd never seen fit to return the favor. There was more to Monty Wilinski than she could learn from old newspaper articles. And until she understood what, she was never going to feel right holding the fate of his legacy—and Mercer's future—in her hands.

MERCER GOT UP EARLY the next morning. He slipped out of Jenna's arms and took a shower, sneaked quietly out the door and jogged to the corner store for eggs.

Jenna shuffled into the kitchen just as he found the whisk.

"Good morning," she said, finger-combing her hair. "Breakfast of champions? I thought you were supposed to just eat those raw."

"I'm making us French toast before I hit the road."

She smiled. "Are you?"

"It's the only thing I know how to cook from scratch. My mom used to make it every Sunday, when she wasn't working."

"Well, I better shower fast, then." Jenna came around the counter to lay a hand on his chest and kiss his cheek.

Mercer caught her fingers, holding them against his heart. "You look beautiful."

She pulled away with an embarrassed smile. "I look like a mess. But thank you."

He let her escape to the bathroom, stealing a peek ten minutes later as she passed by in only a towel. He whistled.

"Shush, pervert."

Mercer smiled, going back to breakfast duties. Not long after, he heard Jenna's voice from her room, unmistakable alarm. "Oh my."

He hurried to her threshold.

She'd dressed for work, hair still twirled up in her towel. Beside her on the bed was the big bin full of photos and keepsakes, and Jenna had a letter unfolded in her hands.

"What's wrong?"

"I was just organizing some of the mess I made last night, trying to get these in order, so I don't miss any...."

"But?"

"I found some other letters, in a paper shopping bag. I started reading one, assuming it was for me. Except the envelope had been slit open already."

"Who was it to?"

She looked up from the page. "It was to my dad. It looks like a Dear John letter, almost. From some woman named..." She checked the envelope. "Lorraine Temple. Did he ever mention her?"

A chill tensed Mercer's back. "I remember Lorraine."

"Did my father date her?"

Her pursed his lips. "They were friends." Or possibly more? It hurt Mercer's heart to imagine it. "Lorraine was... She was his best friend's wife."

He put his hand out and Jenna gave him the letter, standing and crossing her arms. He skimmed it with a thumping heart.

Monty,
You agreed to what I did, that this correspondence has to stop. It's not fair to Frank, and it's not fair to us, either. I'll never forget what you did for him, but you and I... We're over. I'm forever in your debt, and you're forever in my heart. But we can't stay in each other's lives, and you know that as well as I do. The day you won your appeal was one of the happiest of my life, but it's time to leave all that in the past, and start again with clean

slates. I owe you my eternal gratitude, but that's all I have to give. I can't keep sharing my heart this way...

"Did you know this Frank guy?" Jenna asked.

"Kind of. He was around the gym all the time doing pro bono work, accounting or legal stuff. I never paid any attention to the business side of things back then. I can't believe he…" Mercer folded the letter, feeling sad to his very bones. He'd put a lot of faith in Monty, turned him into the father figure he'd missed out on for his first fifteen years. It hurt like hell to imagine him capable of having an affair with his best friend's wife.

"Maybe there's more to it." Jenna sounded more curious than upset, and why shouldn't she be? Monty had never been her father, not the way he'd been Mercer's.

"Maybe." He wanted to hope so, but something in his gut told him not to hold his breath.

"There are more letters in the bag. I'm tempted to read them, to try to understand…but it feels too personal. I don't understand if he left those with my letters because he wanted me to find them, too, or if it was a mix-up."

"I have no clue." Felt as though he didn't have the first clue about anything anymore.

If Monty had been capable of *that,* what about all those other things? The drug-running and money laundering?

What else had his mentor packed up in boxes, hoping to forget, or needing to confess?

And another thing nagged at him. He'd always thought Monty had been somehow *above* romantic relationships, smart to opt out of them after his disastrous marriage to Jenna's mom. Mercer had even thought Monty had been lucky in a way, able to spare himself all the heartbreak love could bring. Too strong to fall victim to that bull.

But love wasn't like drowning, a danger you could dodge

simply by avoiding the ocean. It found you. It had found Monty, after all. No man was safe.

For the past three years, training had been Mercer's priority, the thing he put before sleep, before leisure...miles ahead of his love life, and probably not accidentally.

Then Jenna had turned up and flipped his world inside out. He'd just put his trainee's needs on hold, driven two hours in the dead of night to dry this woman's tears.

Lust or love or whatever this was, he had been right. It was the death of focus, worse than booze. But once you were drunk... Goddamn if bad ideas didn't feel good.

9

JENNA PUT THE LETTER out of her mind as best she could. She had too many letters of her own to process before she tried to make sense of those her father had received from Lorraine Temple. Too much to learn about what he'd felt for her before she could begin to understand something as complicated as an affair.

Plus she didn't want to think about infidelity, not when her own new romance was just blossoming. Mercer had seemed more troubled than her by the letter from Lorraine. His feelings about Monty were more personal than Jenna's, and the revelation surely more upsetting. But by the time he returned from Connecticut, he too seemed to have let the issue go.

She had called her mother on Tuesday evening, prepared to have it out over the way she'd withheld those letters from Jenna. But her anger had fizzled when she heard her mom's side. She'd held on to those envelopes for years, unsure what to do. Admittedly, she'd also been bitter, and she thought she'd wait until Jenna seemed mature enough to handle whatever they held. Then the news of the gym's scandal had broken and she panicked. For all she'd known, Monty Wilinski might've been a dangerous criminal in addition to a bad husband. So she'd made a decision to shut him out for good, and began mailing the letters back. She'd been a scared young mother, only doing her best. Jenna let her resentment go, feeling lighter in its wake.

And for the next week, life was pretty great. Full of hope, excitement, passion…fabric swatches.

The morning of the first Monday in September found Jenna tidying up all the samples the decorator had dropped off, and wishing the office didn't look like such a den of chaos. Mercer had gotten half the filing cabinets moved downstairs, but there were still dusty boxes holding the gym's records from the past three decades stacked in the corners, and old fight posters they'd unearthed from the closet draped over the bookshelves. Then again, Jenna was interviewing prospective assistants all day. Probably best they see exactly what they were signing up for.

She left the office, excited butterflies swirling in her stomach. Down in the gym she found Mercer at work with Delante, showing him some kind of grappling move on one of the mats. She waited patiently until they spotted her and got to their feet.

Mercer grinned. "Hey, boss."

"Hey, Jenna," Delante added. He'd been helping her with random heavy-lifting tasks for Spark, and they'd become friends, of a sort. The sort who had nothing in common, age- or background-wise, professionally… Still, he was helpful and reliable, and the money was keeping his mood level, Mercer said.

"Hi, guys. You can keep going, I wasn't trying to interrupt."

"You nervous?" Mercer asked, knowing full well she was.

Her initial candidate was due at nine-fifteen—the first of six she'd be meeting that day. With the franchise's kickoff mixer less than three weeks away, she needed help, and fast.

Rich swept past, tugging on his sparring gloves. "Hire someone cute."

"That would be a bonus," she said. "Unless she distracts my male clients from the women in the database. Plus I might hire a guy—I have two coming in to interview. Might be nice to have the male perspective on hand."

"You got a whole sweaty basement full of male perspective," Rich offered, and began throwing shadow-boxing jabs in Delante's direction. The two got drawn into a friendly tussle, leaving Jenna and Mercer with a bit of privacy. Well, not that this place was especially discreet. Who could've guessed what shameless gossips professional fighters were? Still, she and Mercer kept it low-key—no "real" kissing in public, just the odd smooch when he swung by the first floor. As for up in the apartment— no holds barred.

"I *am* nervous," she admitted.

"You'll pick the right person. You've got good intuition. I mean you must—look who you keep choosing to hook up with."

She smiled and rolled her eyes. "I'm scared that there just won't *be* a right person. They all look great on paper, but I need that chemistry. And if I don't find it today or tomorrow from the short-list… I'm running out of time."

He rubbed her arm, then pulled his hand away. "Oops, sorry. Just marked you with my territorial musk."

She laughed. "I forgive you."

"You'll be great. Come down at lunchtime and let me know how it's going."

"I will."

He glanced around before planting a peck beside her lips. "Knock 'em dead, Jenna."

BY QUARTER TO TWELVE, she'd had three appointments—two, actually, since the third hadn't bothered to turn up. And the ones that had… She rubbed her temples and poured herself a fresh cup of coffee. Their résumés had looked so promising. The first had been an etiquette coach, of all intriguing things, but in person she came off incredibly fussy, not the sort of woman a client could relax and be him- or herself around. And being one's self was the key to finding Mr. or Miss Right, in Jenna's opinion.

The second candidate was a younger guy, with a master's in psychology. But something about him was…off. Too intense, didn't blink often enough, nodded too vigorously in agreement with everything she'd said. They sounded like niggling complaints, but when someone didn't feel right, they likely *weren't* right.

Her twelve o'clock appointment turned up five minutes early, knocking on the threshold of the open door and not giving Jenna time to hide the packet of peanut butter crackers she'd been mauling.

"Oh, hello." She brushed the cracker flecks from her lap and glanced at her calendar. "Lindsey?"

"Yes. Lindsey Tuttle." The young woman smiled, glancing around the war zone known as Jenna's office.

"Excuse the crumbs. And the mess—we're transitioning. Come in." She leaned over the desk to shake Lindsey's hand. Nice. Firm and confident. "I'm Jenna Wilinski."

"Nice to meet you." Lindsey took a seat in the visitors' chair while Jenna shut the door. She looked to be a couple years younger than Jenna, with wide lips and pale blue eyes, natural dark blond hair pulled into a ponytail. Gray sweater over a dress shirt, pressed slacks. She was cute, with a wry smile, and not *such* a bombshell that Jenna would need to worry about her male clients losing focus. This could work.

Jenna scanned her notes. "So you're currently employed with a wedding planner?"

She nodded. "I just moved here a few months ago, and I've been working for a woman based on Newbury Street."

Jenna had perused the business's website, and the design

had been so slick, she knew only the choosiest, sky's-the-limit brides would be able to afford their services. "Do you like it?"

A guilty smile. "I can't stand it."

"Why not?"

"It's just not what I envisioned. I worked for another wedding planner in Springfield for nearly five years, and they treated me great, let me oversee my own clients. But this job's not what I'd hoped for. I'm really more of a gofer. And more than a bit of a scapegoat when things go wrong."

"Ah, bummer."

"But I promise I'm not here looking for any old job, just to get out of my current one. I'm genuinely interested in the position. Especially the matchmaking."

"What makes me think you might be a good fit?" Jenna asked.

"Well, I know everyone thinks this about themselves, but I'm a really good judge of character. I can meet somebody and within twenty minutes of talking to them, I can get a handle on what they're about."

Jenna believed it. Lindsey had a certain aura about her, something that said, *Your BS won't work on me.* Cold be quite an asset in dealing with pushy or wishy-washy clients.

"And how do you think your background as a wedding planner has prepared you?"

"I've certainly calmed down my fair share of hysterical brides and grooms. I've helped people through what's basically the most important date of their lives, and stripped out all the craziness and the to-do lists, and uncovered what's really at the core of their romance, you know?"

"Go on."

"Well, you'll start working with a bride, and she shows up with binders and folders and printouts, totally caught up in the tiniest little details—the shade of blue she wants for the addresses on the RSVP envelopes. Seating arrangements straight out of a UN meeting."

Jenna laughed, liking Lindsey already.

"It's so easy for women to lose focus in bride-mode. You have to take the time to ask about the relationship they're actually celebrating. Get to the core of what it is that made them love their partner so much they said yes to spending their life with him. And suddenly this bridezilla with her dog-eared catalogs tells you...I don't know. She'll tell you that on her first date with her fiancé, she spilled soup on her dress, and he splashed himself with his wine so she wouldn't feel like such a mess. Something that cuts through the detail-psychosis and reminds them what they're celebrating. Suddenly the color of the seat cards doesn't matter as much as it did before."

"Sounds like you find it very rewarding, at the best of times."

"It is, and I'm good at the planning aspect, but I don't know if it's what I want to be doing five years from now. It was always about the romance for me. And the challenge. I can't tell you how fascinated I am by the idea of matchmaking."

Jenna nodded, thinking she may have just found the perfect match herself.

"Could you tell me exactly what the job responsibilities would be?" Lindsey asked.

Jenna leaned back in her dad's ancient chair, springs wailing. She really needed that office furniture to arrive. "Well, I'm looking for an assistant, like a right-hand woman or man, to help coordinate events and share the load, as the business is getting on its feet. Then once we're officially established, that assistant would still be helping with special events, but also take on their own clients."

"Very cool."

Jenna nodded. "It's appealing that you've already worked with, um, high-maintenance personalities."

Lindsey laughed. "For some of them, that's a kind way to put it. I also grew up as the dead-center of nine siblings, so I'm very well trained at peacekeeping and negotiation."

"Gosh, you could put that on your résumé. Well, it's my hope that my employees won't get stuck working more than a forty-hour week, but in the first year, it's a definite possibility. Do you have other responsibilities that need to be accommodated?"

"None whatsoever."

Jenna saw Lindsey touch her ring finger—wrapping her other hand around it like a reflex. Was she worried her own single status might count against her with Jenna or prospective clients?

"Well," Jenna said, "I worked as an events director on a cruise ship for ages, pretty much on-call around the clock, ten months a year. I'm a firm believer in a work-life balance. So once the craziness of establishing the branch has subsided, it's a priority of mine to make sure my employees feel like their own personal lives are respected, too."

"That's good to know. Though I'm a bit of a workaholic, so I'm not concerned about a little overtime."

Jenna nodded, matchmaker's mind already churning with assessments. Workaholic women often used their careers to avoid romance for whatever reason. She was surely destined to count more than a few of those types among her clients, women who saw "boyfriend" or "husband" as yet another box to check, alongside titled position and stainless-steel kitchen makeover.

But Lindsey wasn't her client, and therefore not her responsibility to analyze. She wasn't even Jenna's employee yet, though she was certainly the frontrunner.

They chatted about day-to-day stuff, and the upcoming mixer. Lindsey had quite a few fun ideas for the event, and tossed out the names of her go-to caterers and DJs. A wedding planner could prove very handy indeed.

When they shook hands—a good fifteen minutes after the time Jenna had scheduled for the appointment—she was smitten herself. Her fears flip-flopped. She no longer worried she might not find someone good enough for the job. She worried the one she wanted might not accept the position.

She had just enough time to run downstairs before her next appointment. Mercer was on his own break, chatting with Rich on a bench while Delante sparred with another young guy in one of the rings.

Mercer smiled as he spotted her and made room beside him. "Hey, good-looking. How'd it go? Any keepers?"

"Oh my God, the most perfect girl ever."

"She cute?" Rich asked.

"Yes, she is, but don't get any ideas. Plus you shouldn't be thinking about women or sex with a big match coming up."

"That's Mercer's sick rule, not mine."

"Anyway, I just hope she'll accept if I offer." She sighed, high with relief, and looked around the gym. It had seemed so intimidating and alien before. Now all she saw was energy, dedication and a brutality she didn't understand but had come to respect since falling so hard for Mercer. She couldn't believe she'd ever been looking forward to the trial period being done, the gym gone. She liked it now as much as she'd resented it for the first twenty-odd years of her life, and it wasn't going down without a fight—hers, Mercer's, everyone's. She wondered if that was why her father had put the stipulation in his will. Maybe he'd known that was all it would take for her to change her mind about the gym—four and a half months. Well, he'd been wrong—it had taken exactly two weeks.

"So," she said. "Everyone on track for the tournament? How long now?"

"Four weeks. And yeah, I'd say so."

She leaned over to address Rich. "What about you, Prince Richard? Feeling confident?"

"Always."

"You could toss Rich in with a guy twenty pounds out of his weight class and he wouldn't blink," Mercer said.

"I love a challenge."

"You love getting hit," Mercer corrected.

"Damn right."

Jenna slapped her thighs and stood. "Better get ready for the next candidate. Just wanted to share the good news. Now I just have to pray she'll say yes when I pop the question."

THE REMAINING CANDIDATES all failed to shine anywhere near as brightly as Lindsey, and two days later, once references had been called and come up sparkling clean, Jenna phoned the woman with her heart in her throat.

"Lindsey Tuttle."

"Hi, Lindsey, this is Jenna Wilinski, from Spark: Boston." She fidgeted with a notepad on her desk. "How are you?"

"Um…frightened," she said with a laugh. "Could you hang on one moment?"

"Sure."

Jenna heard muffled conversation, then when Lindsey's voice came back it was clear she'd relocated, probably out of earshot of her current boss or coworkers.

"Sorry. Thanks. What can I do for you, Jenna?"

"Well, I'm hoping you might come work for me."

She held her breath, but it seemed Lindsey must be doing the same—she didn't reply for several long seconds.

"Oh. Really? Seriously?"

"Very seriously. I was incredibly impressed with you." It felt funny talking this way to a woman only a couple years younger than herself.

"And here I'd been praying for a second interview."

"It doesn't feel necessary to me. Though if you need to ask more questions about Spark before you decide, that's fine. But your old boss from Springfield had very encouraging things to say about you. She's not your mother, is she?" Jenna teased, then went over the salary and benefits briefly, promising to send official information once they hung up.

"All right, then. I accept."

"That's wonderful. Now I have sort of an awkward request. I know you need to give your current work two weeks' notice, maybe longer, depending how your contracts with individual clients work…"

"I don't have any specific obligations to any of the weddings I've been assigned to."

"Two weeks, then?"

"I'm pretty tempted to quit right this minute, but yeah, probably two weeks."

"Would you be interested in making your life a living hell and helping me with some party planning over the next two weekends? All the big stuff for the mixer is in place, but I'd love some help with the nitty-gritty details—email invitations to prospective clients, liaising with the caterer, decorations, security, that kind of stuff?"

"I can do that in my sleep. Just pay me a decent wage and I'll happily run myself ragged for you."

"Excellent. Well, let me get right on all the paperwork, and you email me when your first official day with Spark can be. We'll have another talk about the mixer once all the official stuff is squared away."

A breathy noise came through the receiver. "I'm so excited. Thank you."

"Great. I'll be in touch soon."

"Thanks, Jenna."

They said goodbye, and Jenna felt absurdly happy, as

though she'd just had the best first date ever—a feeling she hoped to give her steadily growing list of clients in the not-so-distant future. A feeling she woke with nearly every morning, the second she registered the warm weight of Mercer's arm slung over her waist.

She let loose a happy sigh, interrupted by the clicking of heels down the front hall. Through the office windows she saw it was Tina, the Spark company's franchise standards overseer. Oh jeez, now? The place was a wreck.

Tina leaned around the threshold and grinned, lips as red as her scarlet suit. "Knock knock."

"Wow, hello." Jenna got up to shake her hand. "Excuse the mess. The gym's manager is still working on getting all his stuff cleared out. You didn't come all the way from Providence just to say hello, I hope?" *Or check up on me,* she thought, though that was the woman's job, after all.

Tina rolled the guest chair over for herself. "No, no. Personal visit—my niece just started at Tufts."

Jenna sat, relieved. "Oh, lovely."

"But," Tina said, expression turning stern. "While I was in town, I wanted to pop in. We've hit a small snag with your space."

Jenna frowned. "Oh?"

"Don't panic—nothing fatal. We're just getting all the *t*s crossed for your branch, and everything's on track, with one tiny niggle."

"Okay."

Tina nodded in the direction of the rear of the building. "That gym."

Jenna's heart thudded. "What about the gym?"

She patted her shiny black updo. "The last time I was here, I couldn't help but notice how…in-your-face it is. Right there, at the end of the foyer. With that big sign over the stairs?"

"Okay." Mercer would just *love* that—some order from on high that now the banner had to come down.

"And what that *says* about Spark. What impression that will give your clients."

"You want the sign gone?"

Tina leaned forward, linking her hands atop Jenna's desk and speaking more quietly. "I was doing some research about the gym and its, shall we say, colorful history."

Jenna's middle gurgled.

"I have to say, as the standards overseer, I've got some major concerns about you sharing a space with a business with such a sordid reputation. Now, I *know* that's not your fault. And I *know* you said you have every intention of closing the business come, what? January first?"

"Yes, b—"

"Great." Tina leaned back in her chair. "That is a *big* load off. We should be fine, as long as the place is closed by the time you're really up and running."

"I'm planning to close the gym if it's *unprofitable,*" Jenna clarified. And over her dead body. "What would it mean for my franchise if it stayed open?"

"Well, I'll be honest with you. It's Spark's profits you really ought to be worried about, Jenna. And having that around—" she poked a finger in the gym's direction "—will not be doing you any favors. Our clients are sharp, discerning, educated people. You can bet they'll be looking into the service they're trusting with their love lives. I'm all for local color, but this is an upscale business. We're already taking a chance on the neighborhood."

Jenna had to bite back a retort. Tina had told her China-town was fine not even two weeks earlier.

"And you can *bet* unhappy clients will be quick to dock you a few stars in online reviews if they find the gym a turn-off. I know it's your late father's name on the place, but it's your name as well. Your client base is going to spike once the mixer happens. Now's the time to have a good long think about appearances."

Jenna's body had gone cold and numb, heated only by a wad of anger burning in her gut. "I'm sure we could come up with some creative ways to mitigate…"

Tina's sad, patronizing smile killed the thought. "I'll give it to you point-blank, Jenna. If the gym doesn't close by the New Year, I can't in good conscience sign off on this space."

"But it was approved months ago."

"And I'm not reneging. There's a perfectly simple solution to this issue, and it's one you seemed only eager to implement when we first spoke. The gym closes, and all our problems are solved."

Jenna blinked at the papers on her desk, choked by the lump lodged in her throat. "Sorry, I just need a second…."

Tina frowned. "I take it your feelings about your father's business have changed since we last spoke about this."

My feelings about my father and, more to the point, the man I'm falling in love with. "They have. Quite a bit."

"That must make this inevitability hard to swallow," Tina said.

More anger flashed. Jenna felt sure the souring in her stomach was the same Mercer had felt when Jenna had shown up, hell-bent on this very same course of action.

"But you need to focus on your own investment," Tina went on, "and I'm the first to tell you, I see big things for Spark: Boston. This space will be great, once the decoration's done. And the rent situation's ideal, obviously. But not with that gym down there. We both know that's not going to fly, right?"

Jenna didn't reply, too worried her anger would be obvious.

"I mean, you wouldn't open a library next to a gun range. Our clients want reassurance, and to feel relaxed. It won't be easy for them to feel at ease with those sorts of people wandering by."

Those sorts of people? Jenna frowned, insulted. But hadn't she thought the exact same thing when she arrived?

"The women will feel intimidated. The men, too. It's just a bad marriage, Jenna. And if there's anything Spark doesn't stand for, it's a bad marriage, right?"

Jenna didn't crack a smile, and Tina dropped the perky approach, speaking frankly.

"Like I said, I like the space. Not the gym. If the gym goes, Spark is still on board. Just a formality."

A formality? Kicking a few dozen guys out of their second home, yanking the jobs from underneath Mercer and the other trainers? How was that a *formality?* How was that anything but a disaster?

"I'll have to talk to the gym's manager," she said, before Tina could pin her down on agreeing that the gym was closing. But short of a miracle...

"Let me know on Monday," Tina said, getting to her feet. "I know you'll make the right choice."

Jenna's chest hurt as she escorted Tina to the exit. As she went back inside her office, she rubbed at her heart, willing it not to ache so much. She shut the door behind her, on the verge of tears.

There had to be a solution. Create a rear entrance for the gym to keep the businesses segregated. Something. Anything.

Anything except closing Wilinski's Fight Academy. That just wasn't an option. Not anymore.

10

MERCER PULLED UP to the curb at Delante's house in Mattapan in the late afternoon. He'd talked a trainer acquaintance from a gym in Allston into letting Delante spar with his strongest heavyweight, and the kid had wiped the floor with the guy. Well, figuratively. Mercer wasn't taking any chances with real injuries, not with the tournament so close.

"Good work, kid."

"Thanks."

"Go get some rest. Don't eat any crap."

Delante exited and grabbed his bag from the backseat. "Later, Merce."

"My best to your mom."

Making a U-turn back toward Boston, Mercer couldn't remember the last time he'd felt this excited.

Probably when he'd gotten his first paid fight, still a dumb twentysomething, convinced he had what it took to be the next big thing. But he knew better at thirty-four. He'd never been half the fighter Delante was. And he'd never felt this… this *pride* in somebody before. This must've been what Monty felt, driving back from a successful match with him or Rich or any of the other kids from Wilinski's.

If Delante or Rich did indeed hit it big, win their upcoming matches and score major contracts with one of the MMA organizations, it wouldn't fix everything overnight. The gym would have a reputable name or two as alumni, always great for attracting new members and maybe even some sponsorship. That might get their monthly balances out of the red, but it wouldn't fund any of Mercer's big plans for the place, not for ages. But he had Jenna on board, and for the first time since she'd turned his world upside down, he felt positive again.

And for the first time since he'd passed, Mercer felt as though maybe Monty hadn't made a mistake, leaving him in charge.

The sun was dropping below the buildings when he pulled into his parking spot in the alley behind the gym. He wondered if Jenna had eaten yet. Maybe she'd like to grab something with him. His day had already been a success, work-wise. Add to that a date and another taste of that crazy chemistry they had…?

After he locked his car, Mercer had to fight off an urge to sprint for the door. He wanted to see her. This was more than chemistry, more than a fling. It was way too soon to say it was anything bigger than a crush, but it *was* bigger than just the sex. It made him feel too many other things aside from lust. Made him feel excited and protective, possessive at the thought of her flirting with some other man, some button-up business guy or trendy designer-type, whatever sorts of men would be sitting down in that office to meet with her.

His pulse thumped harder as he pushed in the door to the foyer. He'd never registered such an urge to win, as if he'd stepped into the ring with his worst enemy, but the competition was romantic. No wonder people did such stupid shit for love, if this was how it made them feel.

The office was locked and dark, so after a quick trip downstairs to make sure Rich was all set with the evening session, Mercer headed up to the apartment.

He unlocked the door, a grin already overtaking his lips, but it died the instant he walked into Jenna's room and found her doubled over at the edge of the bed.

She glanced up just long enough to acknowledge him, and for her tear-streaked, pink face to break his heart. He took a seat beside her and rubbed her back.

"What's wrong?" *Who can I hit to make you feel better?* his inner caveman demanded to know. *Just tell me and I'll find him.*

She raised her head with an undignified sniffle and wiped at her cheeks.

"Tell me what's wrong."

After a few deep breaths, she managed to say, "The Spark standards overseer came by today. She won't approve the space as it is."

He frowned. Did that mean Jenna would be leaving? Something twisted in his chest, different than the pleasant knot he'd just been feeling there. "How come? The area?"

She wiped her eyes, finally seeming to get a proper breath. "No. The gym."

Mercer's heart dropped to his gut. "Because it'll look bad to clients?"

"That's the gist. Because of its history. Because it's supposedly got one of Boston's most infamous criminals' name plastered right over the door."

Mercer's temper flared, but he tamped it down.

"I spent the whole afternoon tracking down the property manager," Jenna said, "to find out if a separate entrance could be put in, so we wouldn't have to share the same one. Like I could even afford it without a huge loan. But the building got historic status a few years back—cosmetic improvements only. I can't do anything to the infrastructure. It was the only half-decent idea I had."

A week ago Mercer's hackles would have shot up to hear

someone denigrate the gym, but the thought passed through his head without stirring a thing. All he cared about was that this woman was crying.

He registered what this meant, of course. The gym was officially dead, as of January first.

He stroked her hair, feeling heavy and exhausted and the thing he hated most—powerless. "That sucks."

She nodded. "Yeah. It does."

"You've been dealing with this all afternoon? I wish you'd called me."

"I wanted to wait until I knew for sure that I couldn't fix it."

The gym, gone. For real. All chances up in smoke.

Come the tournament at the end of the month, Delante and Rich would likely be gone, too, off to pursue better prospects. Mercer would've been stuck here, keeping the gym's heart beating until it all came to an unceremonious, inevitable end, until he shut the lights off for the final time in four months or four years—whenever the money had finally run dry. That wasn't the way this place was meant to go out. Maybe this was all for the best. Mercer felt a sting in his eyes and squeezed them shut until it passed.

"You had dinner yet?" he asked.

"No."

He left her to grab a Chinese take-out menu from the kitchen, and jotted down Jenna's request.

"I'll be back in twenty."

The restaurant was half a block away, and Mercer placed their order then walked to the liquor store for a bottle of wine.

Jenna was still on her bed when he got back, but she joined him at the dining room table, where they ate in near silence, neither acknowledging what her news signaled. He poured her a glass of wine and they turned on the TV, still not speaking. At long last, he couldn't stand it any more—not the elephant in the room, or letting her suffer this way.

"Don't feel guilty," he said quietly.

She met his eyes with her teary ones. "How can I not?"

"It's better to know now, instead of throwing more money at the leaks when the gym's doomed to go under, sooner or later. Sooner's better. Sooner's a mercy."

"It doesn't feel that way. Not anymore. And not since I found those letters…. I don't know what to think of my father anymore. Or the gym."

"I'm sure."

"I know he wasn't the best guy. But I had him so wrong in so many respects."

Mercer felt queasy, remembering that letter he'd been working so hard to put out of his head this past week.

"And I mean, you must feel *awful*. I don't know how you can even stand to sit next to me right now."

It wasn't easy, that was true. But not because he resented her. His being here only seemed to make her feel worse.

They watched TV for a little while, then Jenna sighed, rubbing her face.

"You okay?"

"Calmer, I guess. But I feel so awful. I think I need to read a few more of my dad's letters." She was calling Monty "dad" now, Mercer realized.

He decided to leave the two of them alone. He had a ton to process, too, and that was done best with gloves on his hands. Just after ten, he excused himself to head down to the gym. Members were spraying bags and gloves with disinfectant, mopping sweat off the mats and swiping their membership cards at the desk as they headed home. Mercer clapped them on their shoulders as they said good-night, and found Rich gathering equipment near the rings.

"Hey."

Rich turned. "Oh, now you show up, once all the work's done."

"You wanna train?"

Rich grinned. "Always."

They finished up the nightly chores, then Mercer shrugged into a chest guard and pulled on headgear, strapped thick target pads on his hands as he met Rich in the octagonal ring. They circled each other, Rich tossing out a few lazy warm-up combinations and roundhouse kicks.

"Five minutes," Mercer said, checking the clock.

"Easy."

Mercer raised the pads to shoulder height and flicked one forward. Rich caught it with a nasty hook.

Jesus, he could hit. Mercer had been eighteen when Rich had showed up. Twelve years old, ninety sinewy pounds of seething anger straight out of Lynn, Massachusetts, with a gigantic chip on his shoulder and the cuss-riddled vocabulary of a middle-aged townie. Sixteen years of boxing and later MMA had draped his frame in pure muscle and turned his temper into drive, but Mercer caught old glimmers now and then— that pissed-off kid from the rough end of the North Shore. He'd be seeing more than glimmers in a minute when he told Rich the news. He'd feel it in every punch the guy threw.

"Don't burn it all up front," Mercer said. "Four more rounds."

"Make it ten."

"I need to tell you something."

Whap. "Shoot."

"The gym's gonna close. In January." They'd had this talk a couple weeks ago, but that had been back when Mercer was still determined, and Jenna had the power to decide.

Rich dropped his hands. "What?"

Mercer kept the pads up. "It can't be justified, not the way it's bleeding money every month."

"Bullshit." *Whap, whap whap whap.* "It's not your call, anyhow. It's Jenna's now, and you said she was on our side."

"It's not her call, not anymore—it's some stipulation her bosses at the matchmaking company are laying down. She just found out."

"Oh. *Oh*." *Whap.* A hard one, heavy enough to drive Mercer back a step.

"Watch it."

A dirty hook nearly ripped the pad off Mercer's hand. He kept his guard up. "It would've happened anyway, sooner or later."

Rich's smile was a joyless, ugly thing. "I don't even know who the hell I'm talking to right now. The gym's got to close and you're just, what? Rolling over and letting it happen?"

"I don't have any choice."

"The hell you don't." Rich kept his fists to himself, dancing on the balls on his bare feet. "Monty may have made you the GM, but I'm invested in this place, same as you. I'll *fight* for this place, same as you should. But you're not even going to try, just because you're suddenly getting some—" Rich stopped himself, but Mercer knew which word would've come next. He was half a heartbeat from yanking the pad off his hand and giving Rich a fresh black eye to match the first.

"She's his daughter," Mercer said. "You think it's easy for me to even know how to feel about her?"

"*You're* his kid." He threw a punch that knocked Mercer off balance. "She's just some girl who ignored him for two decades. Now she shows up when she's got something coming to her."

"Watch it," Mercer warned again.

Without fair warning, Rich knocked him back a pace with a kick to his padded ribs.

"What do you even care?" Mercer asked. "You'll be off in a couple months, with a manager. And Delante. The rest of us—" Another mean kick, and Mercer swore. "There's other gyms," he finished.

"There's other chicks." *Whap.* "You've known her for, what, two weeks? You just let her disassemble the place that's been your home for half your life?"

"This place was done already. Maybe we'd have hung on for another year or two, but we were going under, either way. Maybe it's—"

"It's not better this way." *Whap.* "We had a chance. We got our name on a decent tournament, and for what?"

"It's her business, not ours."

"Not ours? Not ours, when we're the ones who've been here sweating our guts out for how long?"

"He left it to her. Not us."

"And if she was any other person in the world, you'd be fighting this, tooth and nail."

"Exactly what legal right do you think I have to stop her?"

Rich shook his head and spoke through panting breaths. "Sit back and let this place close… In six months there'll be some fancy health club down here. A goddamn yoga studio. On the off-chance you and her are still into each other then… you think you can walk in that door and see some other business here? And not hate her? Just a little bit?"

On the off-chance. Mercer winced. On the off-chance she didn't meet someone else, or break things off out of guilt. "I'm not going to try to mess with her plans. I'm standing down. I know you hate it, but that's my call."

"Yeah," Rich panted, finally tiring. "I didn't drive him to dialysis every damned day for a year. So yeah, maybe it's your call. But don't make the wrong one, just 'cause some girl's got you thinking with your dick."

Or my heart. "She's his daughter," he said again.

Rich dropped his hands and Mercer lowered his guard. For a long moment they glared at each other, breathing heavily in the eerie quiet of the gym.

"You got a dad out there someplace," Rich said.

Mercer frowned. "Someplace."

"I had one till the coward shot himself. Now, tell me either one of us would put our biological shithead fathers' wishes before Monty's."

"That's different. He loved her."

"She never returned the favor."

Mercer was tempted to defend her, tell Rich she'd been cheated out of a chance to reciprocate. But it wasn't his secret to share.

"This is what Monty would've wanted." Mercer yanked the pads off and tossed them against the ring's chain-link wall.

"Four more rounds," Rich said.

"Hit a bag. I'm done."

The world had dealt him too low a blow already today. He wasn't taking any more from Rich, not in this mood. "We keep this to ourselves until the tournament's done. Last thing I need is Delante losing his focus."

"Tell me this," Rich said. "She upset about this development?"

Mercer looked him dead in the eyes. "She's upstairs crying. So yeah, she's upset. If that makes you feel better."

Almost imperceptibly, Rich's posture softened.

Mercer shed the rest of his gear, leaving Rich to clean up. On his way out he gave a heavy bag a whack, its chain jangling like sleigh bells.

"He'd never roll over and just let this place close. Not like this," Rich called after him, though the hardness had left his tone.

Maybe it would seem that way to a guy who'd only known Monty the trainer and mentor. Mercer knew another man from that final year, up in that apartment and in those peroxide-stinking hospital rooms. He'd seen him weak and crying, and he'd heard his regrets, listened to them like a chaplain taking final confessions. He'd listened to all the do-overs Monty had never gotten the chance to make, the penances he'd wished he'd paid.

And he knew what he'd want. And where his true loyalties lay.

Jenna started at the click of the dead bolt. She'd carried the bin full of letters to the couch, hoping the words her father had written all those years ago would give her some solace. Let her know it was okay for things to happen this way. But all they'd done was make her feel more confused. She slid the latest letter back inside its envelope, checking the postmark date and finding its correct place in the stack she'd already gone through. Funny how this careful organizing did nothing to lessen how messy everything felt.

She mustered a smile as Mercer entered. He didn't look to be in any shape to return it.

"Did you spar?"

"Kind of. I let Rich wail on me. You find any peace of mind?"

She shook her head. "Not really. It's made me less sure about…about what to do."

"What to do?"

"Like, do I just let the franchise people make this decision to shut down the place he put *decades* into? Is my business really more deserving than his—than *yours*—when it comes down to it?"

"Oh, Jenna." He took a seat and pulled her close. "He'd never have wanted you to sink all your savings into something you cared about, move your whole life here, then just throw it all away so the gym can stagger on toward bankruptcy. I know he wouldn't."

"The more of those letters I read, the less I feel like I have the first clue what he'd want. I just wish it mattered, all those things he wrote. But the overseer isn't going to change her mind just because my dad was some secret softie."

Mercer rubbed her back. "If your dad was here, he'd put your plans first. He never got a fair chance to show you he cared, but if he had this one, he'd take it."

"Maybe." She turned to Mercer, tracing his ear and cupping his neck, her chest aching to know all this intimacy would be over as quickly as it had begun. The grief hit her hard, hot tears slipping down her cheeks.

He smoothed her hair, making a shushing noise. "At least the uncertainty's over. Why are you crying?"

Because... Scary words came to mind, making her panic. She stroked his hair and neck. "I care about you. And I know you care about that place."

"I care about the guys I train. But I can do that anywhere. Work for some other gym, where I won't have to split my energy between being a trainer and a general manager and accountant and every other thing. And your dad would want this, for you."

She blinked, sinuses stinging anew.

"*I* want this for you," Mercer added. He laughed again, a soft, nervous sound. "You've gotten way under my skin since we met."

A fat tear slipped down her cheek, and Mercer brushed it away with his thumb, then kissed the spot. He kept his face there, exhalations warming her jaw. She stroked his head. *Will you move away?* she wanted to ask, but how could he possibly know that yet? How could he possibly be thinking so rationally, when he'd just invited her to turn his entire life inside out?

They sat quietly for a few minutes, playing with one another's fingers, lost in their own heads. Jenna's heart ached from a dozen things. Gratitude and guilt and...love? She felt something like it for Mercer, its soft edges sharpened by his newness and their sexual connection, all that deep affection made electric by attraction. Only a fool would call that love, though, after a couple weeks' acquaintance. She'd never advise a friend to take that first glow of infatuation too seriously, and she ought to listen to that advice herself. *Give it a few months,* she'd say. But as she toyed with his strong, rough fingers, she knew a few months was likely all the time they'd get. And whatever this was, she'd never felt it before.

Mercer excused himself to take a shower, and Jenna began tidying up her father's letters. As she stacked a cardboard box inside the tub, her gaze caught on that paper bag full of letters that chronicled a very different, if equally complex, relationship.

"Why did you include these?" she murmured. Had he meant for her to find them?

She slid a random envelope from the bag.

Dear Monty,
Everything you said, and more. It's been six days since
we said goodbye in Hyannis, but it feels like ages...

Blushing, Jenna set that one aside after a quick skim. It must have been from early in their courtship.

Their affair. The date put it at twelve years earlier, before the criminal scandal had gone down. The next was much the same, and one thing became clear—her father and this woman had been madly in love. Secretly, it seemed, and not without a shadow of guilt lurking behind the effusive, romantic proclamations. The next letter caught her attention. It was short, and there was something cautious about the way it was written...suspiciously vague.

My dearest Monty,
If you love me, you'll do what we talked about. My chil-
dren need their father. I'm a proud woman, but I'll get
on my knees and beg for this. For my family. I risked
everything for what we had, and now I'm asking you
to do the same.

It was signed only as *L*, and Jenna noted the envelope was missing a return address. She had to squint to make out the date stamp. A few months before her father's trial. She shivered.

She heard the bathroom door open and the fan switch off.

"Mercer. Come here a second."

He joined her, towel wrapped around his waist. "What's up?"

"Read this."

She watched his hazel eyes zig and zag across the paper then turn glassy.

"Do you think…? What *do* you think?"

He set the letter down, blinking. "It sounds like she asked him to take a fall."

"Do you think there's a chance he never even knew? If maybe her husband was doing all that criminal stuff without my dad ever knowing?"

"It's possible."

Jenna slumped back against the cushions. "The more I find out about him, the more confused I feel."

Mercer, on the other hand, looked strangely placid. "Give me half the letters. We'll read them together."

She slid a slim stack of envelopes out of the paper bag and divided them. As the two of them read, they paused to share aloud any bits that seemed to pertain to the crimes. The story began to gel, leaving Jenna with conflicting emotions.

She felt sad. For her father. He'd clearly loved this woman, enough for their secret affair to have lasted nearly three years, to judge by the postmarks. They'd escaped on short getaways, away from the city, and Jenna inferred from a couple letters that Monty had occasionally lent her family money. Her husband didn't seem to have been the most reliable provider. When Monty had eventually realized her husband had been using his role at the gym to distribute illicit drugs and launder the money through the books, things had gotten complicated. But eventually, his decision became clear.

> *Monty,*
> *What you're doing... I can't begin to express my grati-*
> *tude. Or Frank's. He'd be the first to admit he's earned*
> *his share of regrets, but because of you, being taken*
> *away from his children won't be one of them. I always*
> *knew you had a good heart—it's what made me fall in*
> *love with you. I never could have imagined you'd risk*
> *your reputation, your business, your very freedom...*
> *But don't lose faith. If there's any way to keep you out,*
> *we'll find it.*

And they had. The letters didn't spell anything out explicitly, but Frank Temple must have had connections somewhere up high—or the funds to create some—as the evidence against Monty had ultimately been mishandled and thrown out, his name cleared on paper if not in people's minds.

Jenna had to wonder why he'd taken the heat. Because Lorraine had asked him to, or because he had so much less to lose? Or because he'd loved her.

"This is the last one," Mercer said, squinting at the envelope. "Jeez. It came way later—only last winter." He read it silently, then passed it to Jenna.

Dear Monty,
You are persistent, aren't you? Almost ten years since I've replied, and yet your letters just keep coming. But of course this time, I had to write. Your condolences and the flowers were much appreciated. I know if Frank hadn't gone so suddenly, he'd have wanted to reconnect. And apologize. But he was always proud, I'm sure you know that.

I hope you're doing well. I'm going to be moving in with my daughter and her new husband for a while, but I'm not going to share the address. I've put Frank to rest, and it's time you did the same with your feelings. I loved you as best I could, for as long as I dared, but please. Don't keep writing.
Best regards,
Lorraine

She set it aside. "Jesus."

Mercer checked the date again. "Your father was already really sick then. He must not have bothered to tell her."

"That's so sad. All the letters he must have sent her…and me. Never getting anything back. That's so…lonely." A sob bucked her shoulders and Mercer hugged her as the tears flowed anew.

He stroked her hair. "He was surrounded by guys who idolized him. He just didn't have such great luck with women, I guess."

Jenna pulled back, rubbing her eyes. "He really was innocent. And nobody believes it."

Mercer smiled weakly. "I did."

She laughed, the sound swallowed by a hiccup. "Yeah, you did. And now I do…."

"It's all in the past anyhow. But at least you got some closure."

"What if...?" She pursed her lips, thinking. "What if this changed things? What if I went to the standards overseer and explained...?"

"None of this will change the legacy the press wrote about your dad."

"No, but she's a cofounder of Spark." It was a long shot, and Jenna felt so manic just now, she knew she'd need to examine it again in the morning, but still. A long shot was still a shot. "She must believe in romance, and in the stuff people do when they love someone. She's human. Maybe I can talk to her, appeal to her sympathetic side...." It meant too much not to count for *something*.

"You can try," Mercer said.

"I will." Jenna sat up straight. "I'll call her first thing tomorrow."

11

JENNA SWITCHED OFF her phone and laid her head on her desk, the ultimate death knell of Wilinski's ringing low and mournful in her heart.

A knock brought her chin back up. Mercer poked his head around the office door so suddenly she wondered if he'd been spying. "Hey."

"Hey, come in."

"Your face tells me the verdict's not the miracle you were hoping for."

She shook her head. "'It just doesn't look good.' That's what she said after..." Jenna checked her phone's call log. "After exactly twenty-two minutes and thirty-one seconds of my very best groveling."

"Bummer."

"For a self-proclaimed romantic, that woman has very hard heartstrings."

Try as she might, Jenna hadn't been able to leverage any sympathy out of Tina. Her livelihood was built on first impressions, and no matter how touched she might or might not have been by Jenna's heartfelt revelations about her dad's criminal involvement, the bottom line stayed the same. *It just doesn't look good.*

He came over and sat on the edge of the desk, circling his palm over her back. "You tried. And that's all you could've done."

She nodded, wishing she felt half as resigned about the situation as Mercer. Her mind raced with ridiculous schemes, to take this story to the news and exonerate her dad publicly... But that was nuts. It was too personal a story, too long buried, affecting too many people.

It was time to give up.

She needed to get her shit together, quit moping and do what *was* within her power—make her business successful for herself and Lindsey and her other future employees and their clients.

"I've got sessions till one," Mercer said, standing and kissing her temple. "But if you can stand a late lunch, maybe I'll see you upstairs? One-fifteen?"

"Lindsey's coming in at three to help me with some event-planning stuff, but sure. There's still lasagna leftover."

"Excellent." He kissed her again, giving the back of her neck a gentle squeeze. "It's a date."

She watched him go, wishing she was half as strong. She hurt so much, she thought it must be ripping her in half, but it was Mercer whose hopes were officially dashed. How he could even stand to look at her, let alone kiss her...

There went one hell of a man.

MERCER GATHERED THE DISHES when they finished their lunch.

Delante had weaseled his way out of training that afternoon, busy helping his sister move into her new dorm and leaving Mercer at loose ends. He didn't do well with loose ends, didn't care for this dangling sensation. Normally he'd fill the void with admin chores, but it was hard to muster the energy for busywork with the gym's demise so official.

He glanced at Jenna. Her blue eyes were aimed out the living room window, chin propped on her hand. Jesus, he'd miss her when he moved on. He'd miss her as badly as he missed her dad, which was insane, given he'd only known her, what? Three weeks? Crazy.

He could stay in Boston. Stay close and keep seeing her for as long as she was into him.

But how long would that last? He was a novelty—a sweaty, bruised novelty, appealing to the bad-idea center of her libido—and that appeal would fade sooner or later. She'd be spending the foreseeable future with successful, clean-cut men marching through her office door like a bachelor buffet. She'd eventually spot someone who was a better fit for her. A guy whose ambitions lined up with hers, whose interests matched, whose career didn't make her wince and whom she didn't feel indebted to out of guilt.

Or was he just making excuses, because this whole thing had him so terrified?

If she did break things off with him, it was a blow Mercer would see coming a mile off. It wouldn't surprise him, wouldn't knock him down. Might leave him reeling for a time, but he'd get over it. He'd get over her. Sure, the idea of another man kissing her made him want to burn the whole damn city down, but hey, what could you do?

But he was wasting the time they did have.

He loaded the dishwasher and dried his hands, then rounded the counter to stand beside her at the table.

"You okay?" he asked, rubbing a fingertip along the crease between her brows.

She smiled sadly. "Just feeling melancholy."

"You have an appointment to get to downstairs?"

"Not until three."

He wound a lock of her hair around his fingers then tucked it behind her ear. "You wanna have a coffee, maybe just sit on the couch and watch TV for a little while? I could stand to clear my head, if you can spare the time." And he wasn't exactly eager to go back to his gloomy subterranean office right away, not when finding a resale company for the gym's equipment was first on his to-do list.

"That'd be nice. Can we watch a trashy talk show, and feel better about our own lives?"

He laughed. "Sure. If you let me get to first base during the ads."

She bit back a smirk, filling Mercer's chest with sweet relief.

"We'll see."

He made a quick trip to his room, then took the reins on coffee duty. He'd finally gotten the hang of her delicate-looking French press, and once the brew was steeping, he carried it and two mugs to the coffee table and plopped down beside her. Already his body was formulating ingenious ways to snap his brain out of its funk. And remind him that what he and Jenna had was great, even if it wouldn't last. Simple. Instinctual. Jesus, she smelled good. What was that?

She took his hand in her free one, resting it on her thigh, and gazed at the flipping channels. He kept his eyes on the screen, registering how she felt, warm and close and now so familiar. Was she holding his hand for the friendly comfort of it? For security? Selfishly, he hoped not. He scooted closer, freeing his fingers and placing them squarely on her thigh, rubbing. Inching higher.

She turned to look at him, lips pursed. "First base, you said?"

"We can go to second, if you prefer."

She laughed. Damn, what a noise. She waved the remote at the droning TV. "There's no ads on right now."

"We could get a head start."

She smiled at him, eyes crinkling. "Okay, then."

They shifted to face each other and he took her jaw in his

hands, kissing her lips. Felt way too easy. Way too perfect. In seconds flat they were making out, the act as exciting and new and fun as when Mercer had been a teenager. He released her face to slip his hand under her skirt and palm her bare thigh.

"That's definitely second," she murmured against his lips.

"I'll steal third, if you let me."

"Yes, I'm sure you would." Still, she didn't push his hand away or tell him to knock it off. God help them if afternoon trysts were suddenly on the table. Both businesses would fail within the week from sheer neglect.

He tugged at her thigh and she took the hint, straddling his lap. He pushed her skirt up her smooth legs, letting her take the lead on the kissing, since he was suddenly too distracted to drive. More suggestions from his bossy hands, and she was seated firmly against him. He pictured the underwear he'd watched her put on this morning—they'd woken in her bed— pale green with some lacy nonsense trimming them. He liked that lacy nonsense. He ran his hands up even higher, finding the material with his fingertips.

"I bet that coffee's ready," she teased.

"I bet you're right." He shifted his hips, letting her know that far more interesting things were also feeling ready. The movement earned him a little sigh, a curious adjustment of her legs. He stroked his palms over her butt beneath the hem of her panties, memorized her cool, smooth skin. She shifted suddenly, leaning over to yank the curtain across the window behind the couch.

"You just made the lowly office drones across the street very sad."

"No free shows. Except for the two of us."

"A worthy trade-off. Should I get a video camera? Is it going to be good?"

She whapped his arm.

Mercer grabbed her by the waist and turned her, laying her

down along the couch. He felt fond flirtation darken to lust as he settled between her legs, her skirt pushed up to her hips. He reached between them to open the fly of his pants, shove his waistband down and take himself out.

She ran her nails over his scalp. "I think you're forgetting something important."

"No way. This was all totally premeditated." He found the condom in his pocket, bracing himself above her on one arm as he ripped the plastic open with his teeth.

"Schemer," she said, stroking his shoulder beneath his T-shirt.

"You ready?" he asked.

"I think so."

He slid the latex down his erection then pushed the strip of her panties aside and ran his fingertips across her core. He found her wetness, slicking it over her lips and clit for a full minute, just to feel her writhe. When the stroking hands on his hips began to tug, he angled himself and pushed inside.

He moaned. They were *way* too good at this. And it was so much better than coffee.

"Good?"

"Yeah. Perfect." She pushed his pants down a little, tugged the crotch of her panties further to the side. Perfect indeed—a hasty, perfect mess. "God, take this off," she ordered, pulling at the hem of his shirt.

He paused only long enough to obey, liking this feeling, him more naked than her, her all dressed up… He was going to develop some weird hot-for-the-boss kink if this kept up. Her hands were all over him in that funny, greedy way she got, as if they were possessed by some secret version of Jenna, one with no shame when it came to enjoying a man's body. And a secret part of Mercer liked that his body seemed to please her, especially when she'd been so skeptical of his chosen sport. Fighters, one. Businessmen, zero.

He braced himself on one arm so he could rub her. It earned him a curse—a word he'd never heard her utter before. He laughed.

"You feel so...*effing* good," she reiterated carefully.

"Don't clean up your language on my account. I like driving you to cusswords."

"We really can't let this become a thing. Afternoon delight's got to be bad for business."

"And for the upholstery."

She smacked his arm again, failing to bite back a smile. Holy shit, she looked perfect—this beautiful, fascinating woman, smiling beneath him, sharing this pleasure.

"But if it never happens again," Mercer said through panting breaths, "we better make this one transgression count."

She gripped his biceps. "I thought this was a quickie."

"Well, we'll make it count effort-wise, if not longevity." He didn't have much staying power in him. Not when she was smiling at him that way, hair mussed, face all flushed. "I kinda need my arms here," he added pointedly.

She took over rubbing her clit, something Mercer had gotten pretty damn good at the past couple weeks. He leaned back, one hand holding her hip, the other the back of the couch.

"You look... Gah," she finished, making a silly face. "You look ridiculous. Nobody should look this good." She ran her free palm up and down his stomach.

"Glad this creaky old body's doing me some good."

"It's doing very, very good."

The conversation ended, moans and grunts and sighs—and the occasional swearword—taking its place. Mercer caught himself thinking too much about Jenna. Cheesy, romantic thoughts full of awe, thoughts he'd always figured were a myth Hollywood had invented to brainwash women. He tried to focus only on the physical pleasure, to make sure he was still capable of keeping sex simple. But the mechanics didn't factor. She was woven into the act through and through, so much more than a warm female body that it scared him.

Screw it.

He was attached, and he'd let himself stay attached. Like drinking too much, he'd regret it when the party was over, but so what? He had it bad for her, and if it was going to hurt when he moved away, may as well hurt a hell of a lot. He'd lived through countless fractured ribs and split lips and black eyes and concussions. He could live through a broken heart.

Beneath him, she was coming apart. His awe returned as he watched her, that normally composed and pretty face looking wild, nearly angry. Beautiful.

"Jenna."

He saw the trembling in her hand, felt it inside her. Need finally muscled the gooey thoughts out of the way, and Mercer wanted release. Now. He waited just long enough for her to come down from her orgasm, then he planted his hands on the couch and sped himself home. Palms stroked and studied him, all a blur. He wanted to come apart inside her, get lost and never be found. When the climax came it enveloped his entire body, wrung him out and left him gasping, white spots winking before his eyes.

"Holy shit."

She laughed, rubbing his shoulder.

Blood slowly returned to his brain and he managed to make it to his feet, stumble to the bathroom and ditch the condom. Jenna was running her fingers through her messy hair when he returned, and he studied her fondly as he pulled his shirt back on.

"Thanks for the lasagna," he said.

A smile, nearly as pleasurable as the orgasm. "You're very welcome. Thanks for the sordid quickie."

He returned the smile, wishing to God all this was really as simple as he was pretending it was.

LIFE GOT HECTIC. With both the mixer and tournament drawing near, Jenna and Mercer were seeing less and less of one another as organizing their mismatched events took over the daylight hours. But at night… At night they picked up where'd they'd left off the last time they'd enjoyed each other's company, and that tended to be one of their beds.

Having a wedding planner on staff was a godsend. Lindsey thought of details that would never have occurred to Jenna. With her assistant's help over the next two weekends, the cocktail party was starting to feel as though it really would happen, and that it really would be rather fabulous.

Best of all, Lindsey's old boss had let her go with just one week's notice. She fit in very nicely around the place, Jenna thought. Mercer agreed. The two had hit it off over a harried pizza dinner in the office that Saturday. Only one thing threatened the party's success.

"Any good news on the man-procurement front?" Lindsey asked as they settled into the office on Monday morning. It was her first official day, and five short days before the mixer.

Thanks to the success of the billboards and subway ads, they now had a nice little list of confirmed attendees—some already preregistered with Spark, others eager to make their decisions based on whom they might meet at the party. But the women outweighed the men more than two to one.

"Sadly, no," Jenna said, opening her laptop.

"What would you think about offering the women a discounted month of membership in exchange for bringing along a single male friend?"

Jenna knocked the idea around in her head. "I'm afraid it'd look kind of lame for a matchmaking service to ask prospective clients to BYO men."

Lindsey frowned. "Right, duh. Jeez, you'd think free booze and shrimp would be enticement enough. It's what gets people to go to weddings."

"Doesn't help that men are less prone to scheduling things ahead of time, or replying to RSVPs. For all we know a ton will decide to show up on Saturday—they just won't bother to tell us about it."

"Now that you're stuck with me," Lindsey said, "I feel like I should admit I'm going to make a pretty hypocritical matchmaker."

"How so?"

"I've read the new client orientation materials back to front, and I've got to tell you, I don't adhere to, like, half those rules. If the right guy walks through that door, I give myself one date—maybe two, tops—before I take him for a test drive."

Jenna smirked. She'd yet to go on a real date with Mercer. "That's a strict one, I know."

"Try before you buy," Lindsey proclaimed, rubbing an imaginary stack of bills between her fingers.

Jenna laughed. "If I catch you saying that to a client I'll demote you to receptionist."

Someone walked by the office windows, but Jenna had been inhabiting this room for long enough that she no longer glanced up at every passing shadow. Not unless she felt a little pang of happy queasiness, in which case she could reliably find Mercer on her threshold.

There was a scuffing of shoes and Jenna looked up to find Rich in the doorway.

After news of the gym's imminent closing had been shared with the trainers, Rich had treated Jenna as though she didn't exist for several days, but eventually his cold silence turned to single-syllable exchanges, then to a more authentic imitation of friendliness. And the expression on his handsome face now was far from angst.

Lindsey was distracted, and behind her back Rich gave Jenna an amusing little show. His gaze went from Lindsey to Jenna, then back to Lindsey, brows rising. Jenna rolled her eyes and beckoned him inside.

"Morning, boss. And mystery woman." He flashed one of his dangerous smiles.

"Rich, this is Lindsey Tuttle, my new right-hand woman and future matchmaker. And the person who's going to single-handedly make this mixer happen. Lindsey, this bruised specimen is Rich. Mercer's, um, colleague."

"Nice to meet you," Lindsey said, rising to shake his hand. If the gigantic welt on his jaw or the powerful body not much camouflaged by his sleeveless shirt gave her pause, she hid it perfectly well.

"Rich Estrada," he said. "Light heavyweight, nine and one—though that one was pure robbery." He released her hand and turned to Jenna. "Where've you been hiding this one?"

"This is my first official day," Lindsey said.

"Don't get any ideas," Jenna warned. "I own her every waking minute until this party's over."

"Speaking of ideas," Lindsey said to Jenna, "have you considered inviting the guys downstairs to the mixer?"

"I had, briefly...." She exchanged a not-entirely-easy look with Rich then glanced at the door to make sure no one was passing. "But I don't think they'd appreciate discovering I recruited them for a kickoff of the business that's driving the gym away."

Rich shook his head gravely.

Lindsey's smile drooped. "Of course not. Too bad. Would've been a nice mix, added to all those white-collar types."

"Oh yeah?" Rich made an approving face and crossed his big arms over his chest. "You got a soft spot for scar tissue, sweetheart?"

"It's not a matter of scars or any other thing," she said,

putting on a nice little snob act to counteract Rich's swagger. "And my soft spot is officially off-limits to partygoers."

Rich laughed.

"No matter their fight record or what they can bench. I'm very happily single. And I'm quite happy to focus on other people's love lives for the foreseeable future."

He smirked. "Well, I'll have you know that torture chamber's packed with undercover businessmen and all sorts of boring types. Only a few of us sweat from nine to five. One of our best amateurs is a pediatrician."

Jenna grinned. She knew as well as anyone that the gym wasn't what it seemed. What went on down there was a craft that few outsiders could make sense of, but the men drawn to it went beyond the bloodthirsty and one-dimensional.

"Too bad we're shutting down—Merce was gunning to build a female membership. Could've found out if one of you two was the next big thing."

"Think I'll pass." As much as Jenna now respected the sport and its practitioners, she wasn't inviting anyone to punch her. Lindsey looked more game, nodding with a thoughtful little smirk.

"There's always private lessons," Rich added, bobbing his brows at Lindsey with innuendo.

She rolled her eyes and turned back to the printouts on her desk.

"You'll have to excuse us, Rich," Jenna said. "We have a man-drought to solve."

"I'll leave you to it. I'm late for a scrap with your boyfriend."

Jenna nearly corrected him, but she shut her mouth, because temporary or not, official or not, Mercer was obviously her boyfriend.

Once Rich had bidden them goodbye and disappeared in

the direction of the gym, Lindsey shook her head. "He's a bit full of himself, leading with his fighting stats."

"That's his shtick. Prince Richard."

"Well, they ought to call him the Rooster. He's insanely cocky."

"Seems to work well in the ring."

Lindsey smiled grimly. "Well, it doesn't work on me. I've had it up to here with egotistical men." She drew a line across her throat and made a gagging face.

Jenna could sense the faintest defensive tone behind the silly gesture, and wondered if her assistant might be talking about more than just annoying grooms. An ex, maybe. A *fresh* ex, she bet. But Lindsey was one of the few women who'd arrive in this office *not* seeking Jenna's opinions about their personal lives, and she'd respect that, much as the curiosity drove her crazy.

"Let's take stock," Jenna said. "Catering's done, officially?"

"Ditto the bar service. I went ahead and approved the costs my contact emailed me, because it was pretty much exactly what you'd budgeted."

"Perfect. Security? Oh, that company the franchise overseer recommended. I better call and confirm they're sending us three guys. The only thing we're short on is us, really," Jenna said. "You and me, plus Tina." Tina would be sweeping in from Providence to make sure the party went off to Spark's standards. Jenna felt a familiar surge of dislike toward her boss, but stuffed it back down, knowing the woman's decision had been purely professional…much as it hurt. Plus Tina knew the business inside and out, and Jenna needed her help as much as she feared messing up with Tina as a witness.

"Three people should be enough," Lindsey said. "Also, the hotel said it'll be no problem getting a couple laptops set up so people can register. Oh, and you know what I thought would be fun, and really easy to do, to get people into the mood to join?"

"What?"

"We should print up cards with sample questions from the compatibility survey, the one you take after you join? All those fun questions about, like, what celebrity is your ideal date? What cocktail best sums up your dream man or woman?"

"Right."

"We could scatter them around the tables and invite people to quiz each other. People *love* being quizzed. Especially when they've got a nice wine buzz going. Plus it'll entice people to sign up, so they can take an entire survey about what they want in a mate. I don't want to imply that people are narcissists or anything…"

"No, you're right. That's the most empowering part of joining a dating service, that initial stage where you're focused on what you want. It *is* fun, getting all hopeful and excited about Mr. or Miss Right, feeling like it's all about you."

"So what's left to do? Decorating?"

Jenna nodded. "I've ordered as many floral arrangements as the hotel suggested for that room, and they offered to rent us the tablecloths. But I thought on Wednesday you and I could go shopping for other random stuff to spiff the place up. There's room in the budget for that, thanks to your connections cutting us deals on the food."

"The DJ promised to email me the playlist and cc you. I told him, 'Upbeat make-out music for classy people.'"

Jenna laughed. "Sounds perfect. Jeez, we're actually in good shape. I didn't see that happening this time last week. In fact, on Wednesday, after we're done shopping for extras, I'm taking you to lunch, to say thanks."

"I won't stop you."

"But today and tomorrow, we're focused on man-procurement.

Let's see if we can't get a few of our better prospects to commit. Or at least RSVP."

While Lindsey got busy with that, Jenna sneaked downstairs, thinking she'd see how Mercer's day was.

He wasn't in the gym itself, but the door to the makeshift office—formerly a storage room—was open. She waved to a bunch of fighters as she crossed the floor mats, shoes in hand, to peek around the threshold. Mercer was sitting on an old metal desk under the room's rather harsh overhead light, talking on his phone, the fingers of his free hand drumming the desktop. His face looked ominously, dangerously sexy in the severe glow from above. He didn't see her.

"No, I'm interested," he said. "Full-time, though, right? Great. I'm done here as of January first."

Jenna's stomach constricted. She'd spent the past couple hours with Lindsey, thrilled to see how excited her assistant was about the opportunity Jenna had given her. But on the flip side, she was wrecking the dream job of the man who shared her bed…and heart. Buzz killed dead, she backed away and headed upstairs.

By MID-WEEK, Jenna and Lindsey's gentle email reminders had indeed managed to garner a few more RSVPs from Greater Boston's male population. Jenna had ignored Lindsey's snide suggestion they simply title the subject line "Free Shrimp!" She'd gone instead with "Real Men Wanted." Every guy liked to think of himself as a real man, both in the rugged sense and also the inclusive Everyman sense. It won them over a dozen new acceptances, bringing the total number of confirmed guests to an impressive but manageable seventy, and the ratio to about sixty percent women, forty percent men. Doable.

The trip to find extra decorations had been a success and on Wednesday evening Jenna was camped out with boxes of would-be centerpieces.

The door clicked, announcing Mercer's arrival and filling her with happy, antsy energy. She smiled as he stepped inside. He'd been gone the entire afternoon, taking Delante to a steep hill on the South Shore to run sprints, something to do with lung capacity or some other sadistic fighter-thing.

"Hey, you." He closed the door, looking as exhausted as she'd ever seen him. "What's happening here?"

"Centerpieces for the party. Don't judge yet—they're not done." Before her was a wasteland of vases and glass pebbles and willow branches, soon to be transformed into miniature trees and festooned with the survey question cards Lindsey had printed. "How was torturing Delante?"

"Great. The countdown's kicked in. He's got a healthy fire under his ass now." He stretched his neck and tossed his keys on the coffee table. "Some kids crumble under pressure, but for him, that's what he was missing."

"Excellent."

"Yeah. Now I just need to focus on finalizing all the last-minute crap for the tournament. Too bad I don't have a Lindsey of my own—I'm useless with juggling details. Rich is even worse."

She frowned her sympathy.

"That was always your dad's thing," Mercer said. "Though luckily the promotions company's pretty organized. You eat already?"

"I was waiting for you." She stood and stepped over the mess. "Nothing fancy, pasta and these good sausages I found in the North End."

"I'd eat my own leg, I'm so hungry."

She got dinner ready while Mercer showered. He emerged and walked to where Jenna stood stirring the sauce, and wrapped his arms around her middle. He smelled like soap, and she knew exactly how his wet hair would feel if she turned and kissed him and ran her hands over his head.

She'd arrived here expecting someone so different. Tough and stubborn, an opponent. And here he stood, her unlikely boyfriend. She ached to tell him she loved him. She'd said those words to men she'd been less enamored with than Mercer. Not insincerely, either. She simply hadn't known a romantic attachment could run this deep.

"Smells awesome," he said.

"So do you."

"Compared to my usual stinky man-fragrance, I'm sure I do."

"Get us some bowls and utensils, Mr. Rowley. And the cheese shaker."

"Will you kill me if I watch the Sox-Yankees game?"

"Of course not. I think I'd get excommunicated if I stopped you. Let me clear off the couch."

They settled in the living room, and Jenna liked the atmosphere—each of them absorbed in their own concerns. Mercer's presence felt warm and easy and natural.

The Sox lost, but Mercer almost seemed to relish it. Like Boston itself, he thrived as the underdog. If only that spirit could've somehow saved the gym.

Jenna managed to come up with a decent arrangement for the little card trees, though her fingers were nicked and achy by the time Mercer switched off the TV at ten. She wondered if he'd like to work off his Sox angst in one of their beds.

"I, um…I have some news," he said.

"Oh?" She tensed.

"Yeah." He turned to the side, hugging one of his knees and looking her in the eye. "I think I've secured a pretty damn decent training gig for the New Year."

"Oh," she repeated, numb. "Where?"

"Philly."

The word knocked the wind out of her. *"Philadelphia?"*

"Yeah. Straight-up boxing. Not mixed disciplines. But I

know the guy who runs the gym—he worked for your dad ages ago. Good young prospects to work with."

"That's so far away."

His expression softened, reflecting her own preemptive grief. "It is far. But it's a good fit. And it gets me out of Massachusetts and away from all the old rivalries between the facilities here."

"Right." Wilinski's and its fighters had never quite managed to shed their pariah status, he'd said, and suffered a lot of trash talk for it.

"You okay?"

She nodded. She had to be all right, since it was his decision. Hurt like hell, though. "When do you think you'll go?"

"It's an open invitation. So whenever things get wrapped up here..."

"Right."

He smiled grimly. "Don't go into guilt-mode again."

"I can't help it." And it wasn't only guilt. It was selfish sadness and frustration, this official notice that they'd be breaking up. This proof that whatever he felt for her wasn't enough. For the second time in her life, a man was choosing boxing over keeping her close. Only this time, she was old enough to realize it.

She shook her head. "That's so far away...."

"Listen, Jenna. I'm not talking about this with you. It's what I've got to do, and I need you to just trust and respect that my decision's a good one."

"It has nothing to do with respecting or trusting you. It's about me needing to understand, because...well, because I've gotten awfully attached to you."

His expression softened. "And you know that's mutual."

"We talk about everything else. I can't stand the idea that my plans are driving you all the way out of your hometown."

Your territory, she thought. Like she'd emasculated him, sent him packing off to distant lands to start his ruined life over.

"Well, I don't *want* to talk about this with you, okay?"

"Why not?"

Another sigh, a heavy one, and he stared down at his knee. "Because it'll make you feel bad."

"I feel bad already. Try me."

He ran his hands over his head. "I can't stick around here. I can't be this close to the gym after it's closed. I can't keep seeing you, keep coming over here—certainly not continue to *live* here—remembering how things were before you showed up."

Her mouth dropped open. She felt slapped.

"See? I told you it would hurt. But seriously, once the gym's gone and my entire purpose in this town is finished, coming by here to see you… It'll be like walking past a grave. I want to tell you I'm above winding up bitter about it, but I can't promise that."

"Mercer—"

"What we've got going on, it's great. I want it to end still feeling great, not just for us, but because you're Monty's daughter. I want us to end on a high when I move away. I don't want to stick around here and find out in six months or a year that I resent you, and have what we've got end in some ugly fight. That would wreck our relationship, and the memory of the one I had with your dad. I couldn't save the gym. But I can keep from hurting you, which he would've wanted. And what I want, too."

She wanted to argue with him, but the thing was, he was right. He was being painfully honest with her. She didn't want Mercer to resent her. She didn't want to watch him settle for some consolation, good-enough job in the city, a witness to whatever successes might lie ahead for her. Or worse, to watch her fail in the long run, discovering he'd sacrificed what he loved for nothing.

Mercer was a good man, but only a saint could possibly be asked to do all that and smile through it.

"I understand."

"Good."

"Still sucks, though."

He smiled. "I know. But it'll suck less than an ugly breakup. Or even if we just…fizzled, or whatever."

She doubted very much that something as passionate as the bond they shared could ever just *fizzle,* but she nodded. Perhaps snuffing out their candle *was* the most merciful way to go.

"When we say goodbye, it'll be sad, but we'll still like each other."

Much more than just *like.* "I know." She scooted over to lean against him, laying her cheek on his shoulder. "But it'll still suck."

He stroked her hair and missed the top of her head. "That it will."

12

JENNA STARED BLEARILY at her laptop, headache brewing. She glanced up as Lindsey swept through the door. The office was finally organized, but Jenna couldn't yet say the same about the party.

"Good morning, and happy Mixer's Eve," Lindsey said brightly. It was Friday, the day before the party.

"Actually, I'm afraid it's not such a good morning."

Lindsey frowned and shrugged off her jacket. "No? What's happened?"

Jenna looked at her screen, at the bad news in question. "Our event security's fallen through. I woke up to the email."

"An email cancellation? How tacky."

"No kidding. Apparently the company just folded overnight. Some dispute between the owners. And these are the guys Tina recommended." She sighed. "I don't suppose you've got any go-to security folks?"

"Weddings don't usually call for bouncers. Though some of the ones I've survived really should've considered it."

Jenna rubbed her temples. The fact that she'd been sleeping poorly didn't help her mood much. Two nights in a row she'd gotten perhaps four hours' real rest. The remainder of the time she'd spent lying awake with a possessive arm locked around Mercer, brain stuck on an endless loop of to-do items and panicky calculations of how many weeks remained before the man she loved moved away.

"You think we could get away without it?" Lindsey asked. "It's only a cocktail party."

"Not a chance I want to take. Neither of us is up for playing bouncer, if people break the two-drink-maximum rule and get rowdy."

Lindsey nodded her grudging agreement. "I'm sure we'll find something. It'll just cost. I'll call around first thing."

"No, I'm on it. I've already got a list of possible companies. Though most of the websites want two weeks' notice. We've got less than two *days*. But as soon as this coffee kicks in, I'm getting my groveling boots on. You want some?"

Lindsey nodded and took her seat. "Please. The Green Line broke down on me, no surprise."

"You're right on time," Jenna said, filling a mug.

"Yeah, but I wanted to be early, since it's the eleventh hour. Thanks," she said, accepting the cup. "What do you want me to tackle while you worry about security?"

"Organizing. Confirm when the food and drinks and music are getting there, and make sure the hotel can still send a van to pick us and all those centerpieces up. Mercer offered, but he's busy with his own party of sorts."

Lindsey nodded. "One with paramedics on hand in place of cocktail waiters. Say no more. I'm on it."

"Thanks."

After a pause, Lindsey skirted the desk and patted Jenna's shoulder. "Don't stress. Up until the security thing, we've had amazing luck. Trust me. If nothing had gone wrong by now, I guarantee something would've imploded at the actual party. Something *always* implodes. Now we just know what it is!"

Jenna smiled. Lindsey was a frank and grounding presence. She also had to admit she was anxious about more than the cancellation. She was down about Mercer leaving, and though she tried to tell herself they still had a few months together, that it was for the best… Well, it hurt. A few months was plenty of time for him to start resenting her, the thing they both feared even more than their actual parting.

"I have that appointment with the events person at the hotel at ten-thirty," Lindsey reminded Jenna. "I'll swing by the printing place on the way."

"Do you need petty cash for a cab?"

Lindsey drained her cup in two gulps and grabbed her purse. "I'll walk. It's gorgeous out there."

"Great. See you in a bit."

Barely a minute later, Rich appeared in the doorway. He'd been turning up to say hello with rather tactless frequency since Lindsey had started. That she was thoroughly immune to his charms didn't seem to deter him. Quite the opposite. But he seemed to have forgiven Jenna for the gym's upcoming closure, and she welcomed his shamelessness. It beat angst by leagues.

"She's gone out for the morning," Jenna said, opening a new email.

"Who has?"

She rolled her eyes. "You're not half as smooth as you think you are," she teased. "I hope you're better at poker faces when it comes to your matches."

"The best," he said with a smile. "And I still don't know what you're talking about."

"What can I do for you, Richard?"

"Nothing. Just saying good morning. You all ready for your big party?" He swiveled the guest chair around to take a seat.

"Nearly. Except the security guys we hired fell through this morning."

"Ouch. You really need muscle for a cocktail thing?"

"Probably not, but it's not a risk I'm going to take. Do you know anyone in security, by any chance?"

"Got a cousin who's a mall cop in Peabody, but you don't want to hire him. Trust me. What about us, though?"

"Who? You guys downstairs?"

"Sure. I'd do it. Mercer's, like, in love with you, so he'd do it."

She blushed, praying Rich wouldn't notice.

"How many you need?"

"I booked three, but I think two would do. But come on— we decided not to invite any of you to come to the party because of how rude it would be. Once the gym closes," she added quietly.

"Sure, but me and Merce already know the score. Plus you'd offer to pay us, right? It's not like you're using us to pad the male population. Mind you, we *would* show up all your blue-shirted business-weenies."

Jenna frowned, considering his offer. It'd be tough to find anyone she trusted as much and on such woefully short notice. And she *would* pay them.... But she didn't like the idea of the gym and Spark overlapping this way, or of feeling she was taking advantage of Mercer. "Maybe."

"What maybe? It's totally easy. No classes for either of us to worry about after five on Saturdays. We won't drink. I'm charming as all get-out. Gimme, like, two minutes to talk Mercer into it, and your problem's solved."

"You can't rough anybody up. You can only escort people out if they get drunk, that kind of thing. Very quiet, very discreet. No scenes. Though likely you'll just be bored, standing around all night, watching nervous people flirt."

"Fine. What do we need to wear?"

"Same as the guests. Business casual, but with security badges, I guess. I wonder where I could get those from...."

"I'll find something," Rich said. "Probably a good idea. If we pass for guests, we'll seduce all your single ladies away."

"Well, fine. You're on. If you can pull it off, you're welcome to the gig. We were going to pay the other guys forty dollars an hour—"

Rich waved the notion away. "I only cared that you'd *offer* to pay us. Mercer won't let you, and much as I'd like to think I'll take the money, I probably won't."

"We can argue about that later."

"Great. I love a good fight."

Jenna smiled at him. "Thank you. That's very helpful. I'll need you there early tomorrow. The party starts at seven and goes until ten, officially, probably more like ten-thirty. But you guys should be there at six-thirty, to meet the hotel staff and get a sense of the room, that sort of thing."

"Plenty of time to shower and get gussied up for you."

"Lovely. Thank you, Rich."

"You got it, boss." He returned the chair and headed for the door, turning in the threshold. "What's Lindsey's favorite color?"

"Oh gosh, I don't know."

"Don't women always know that kind of crap about each other?"

"Um, plum, maybe. Her purse and phone are plum-colored."

"What's that—like purple?"

"Very dark purple."

Rich made a thoughtful face and nodded, then disappeared in the direction of the gym.

WITH THE SECURITY CRISIS AVERTED, Jenna spent the rest of the day checking off the final boxes on her mile-long to-do list. At three she finally found the nerve to pick up her phone and make the call that intimidated her the most. She listened to the dial tone, heart pounding in her throat.

"Tina Maxwell."

"Hi, Tina, it's Jenna."

"Jenna, how are you?" That smooth, schmoozy voice. Jenna nipped her annoyance in the bud the second it registered.

"I'm getting nervous," Jenna admitted. "But mostly excited."

"You're going to do just fine. Have you got your welcome speech memorized?"

"Pretty much. I know what I want to say, but I always sound dumb when I just recite, so I'm going to wing it a little."

"Good plan. Tomorrow should be all about conversations. Just talk to your clients like friends, because that's how we want them to feel. Guests at a friend's party. Plus I'll be there. If you start to fumble, I'll step in and praise the heck out of you."

"Sounds good."

"All the details wrapped up?"

"Getting there," Jenna said. "We had one snag with the security company you recommended."

A pause. "Oh?"

"Yeah. They, um, sort of…disbanded."

"Oh my. Have you found replacements?"

"Yes." *Please don't ask who. Please don't ask who.* Tina hadn't come out and insulted the gym members, but they were obviously on the same level as pests in her estimation, above cockroaches but firmly below noisy next-door neighbors.

"I should be arriving around two," Tina said, and Jenna found herself able to breathe again. "I'd love to come by the office and see what you've done. The photos you emailed looked fabulous."

"That should be fine. We're heading to the hotel to set up at three-thirty."

"Wonderful. I'll see you then. Don't hesitate to call if you have any questions or concerns. And let yourself be excited! You're going to do just great."

"Thank you. Oh and Tina?"

"Yes?"

"Don't forget, all the guys who belong to the gym downstairs, they don't know yet about it closing. Only the employees, so…"

"Never fear. This job's made me a walking card catalog of diplomatic details. My lips are zipped."

They said goodbye and Jenna felt that little ball of acid in her stomach. She sighed, just as Lindsey appeared with their very late lunches.

"Toasted sesame bagel with chive." She set Jenna's paper bag beside her computer. "What was that gigantic sigh about? Has anything else gone wrong?"

"No, not at all. Just talked to Tina. Just feeling crappy about the gym closing. I won't bore you with my guilty laments."

"It does suck." Lindsey opened her bag and spread a napkin over her desk. "They're nice guys, all the ones I've talked to. I hope they stay nice, after the bomb drops."

Jenna nodded. She didn't like thinking about that, either. Mercer's reassurances notwithstanding, fighters struck her as a passionate group. She hoped everyone would take the bad news in stride. "We've got Mercer and Rich on our side, at least. They've got a lot of sway."

"Are you going to the tournament?" Lindsey asked, smearing cream cheese on her bagel.

"Probably, yeah. I want to, because it means so much to Mercer, and I'm really rooting for Delante and Rich to win their matches. But I don't like that stuff. Watching people get hurt. Even if it's what they enjoy."

"I looked MMA up online the other night. It's sort of cool. Not cheesy like I expected, like pro-wrestling. It's pretty badass."

"Indeed."

"Then again, I have five brothers who lived and breathed hockey growing up, and played tag like the point was to rip your head off. Fighting doesn't shock me too much. Plus watching live, unless we got really amazing seats…you can't see too much of it, the bloody stuff. Especially not with the cage thing in the way."

"What's this 'we' business?" Jenna teased. "Are you going?"

"Why not? Mercer and Rich are stuck yawning their way through our big night. We should say thanks by wincing through theirs."

"Mercer hasn't even invited me."

"I'm sure it's implied," Lindsey said. "He *is* your boyfriend, whether you'll admit it or not."

"Maybe." Then again, the tournament marked the beginning of the end for their relationship. Once that came and went, the secret would be out, the gym's closing going from a theoretical worst-case scenario to a very real eventuality. She didn't think she'd much enjoy the event with that looming over them. "Maybe."

"I just found out Rich could win, like, fifteen thousand dollars," Lindsey said. Was it just Jenna, or had she mentioned his name just a little *too* casually?

"Yeah. He's nearly a headliner, third-to-last match on the card. I don't know who the guys are who are in the two super-top fights."

"Fifteen grand, for, like, twenty-five minutes' work." Lindsey shook her head and took a bite of her lunch.

"Not twenty-five minutes I'd ever want to take part in. Not for a *hundred* grand."

"I saw videos of him online. Of Rich, I mean. He's a freaking *weirdo.*"

"Yeah, Mercer said he's got an obnoxious ringside manner. Some fighter shtick. Shall I tell him you're stalking him on YouTube?"

Lindsey snorted. "God, no. His ego's inflated enough as it is. I was just trying to figure out how violent the tournament was going to be, to decide if I wanted to go, and his was the only name I knew to look up."

"Ah." Jenna nearly believed her. Nearly.

"Oh, you know what we forgot?" Lindsey said, setting her bagel aside.

"No. What?"

"Name tags."

"Oh, crap—"

"Don't panic. I found some awesome ones at Paper Source." She leaned over and picked up her purse, fishing out boxes and handing them to Jenna. "I got a hundred, just in case. Pretty nice, huh?"

She studied the stylish stickers and the silver pens Lindsey passed her. "Yes, very. And good catch."

"I'm so excited. I can't wait to chat with people and steer them toward possible matches. Diplomatically, of course."

"And draw the shy ones in, too," Jenna said. "Tina told me that can be an issue. Letting people hang back is awkward for everybody, so we have to take the lead on them. But I've peer-pressured more than a few wallflowers into socializing during my cruise days. I'm sure we'll be fine."

Lindsey sighed, a happy noise. "It's so much more fun dealing with other people's social lives. Like all the fun of baking and eating a cake, with none of the cleanup to worry about."

Jenna snorted. "Oh, we'll have plenty of cleanup before long. Plenty of 'Why did you set me up with *that* loser?'"

Lindsey made a face. "Yeah, true. Except we'll be unnaturally perfect at all this. The only dating agency in the history of forever with a one hundred percent client satisfaction rate."

"I admire your delusion," Jenna said, laughing. "And sharing it might just get me through tomorrow's party."

At ten to two on Saturday afternoon, Jenna spotted Tina strolling past the office windows and her nerves rose from a steady simmer to a rolling boil. No time to even smooth her hair, she set aside one of her many lists and got to her feet.

"Jenna!" Tina beamed a broad smile around the office, seeming to approve of the changes Jenna had made since she'd been here for the official inspection. "Foyer looks fantastic. I even sat in the chairs. Very comfortable. I might suggest a watercooler, though."

Lindsey waved from her chair and wheeled it forward. "Hi, I'm Lindsey Tuttle. Jenna's assistant-slash-future-matchmaker."

"Yes, Lindsey the wedding planner." Tina's shake looked as crisp and professional as her gleaming bun. "Lovely to meet you. Jenna's been absolutely aglow with your hire. Welcome to Spark."

"Thank you. And for the foyer, I was thinking maybe we could set up a little table with one of those fancy one-cup coffeemakers."

"That sounds like a great idea," Tina said.

"Lindsey's full of those," Jenna said. "So here's the office." Lindsey gestured cheesily like a boat-show model. "It's not done, clearly, but all the furniture's in. I've been trying to figure out what color to paint the walls, since we've got to appeal to men *and* women."

Tina aimed an appraising eye around the room. "I'd suggest something dark. Soothing. A dark slate, to offset the pine?"

Jenna made a note. "We'll get swatches next week, once everything's calmed down."

"I'll bet you're looking forward to the party wrapping."

"I'm excited for the mixer itself. But yeah. I'm ready to meet my clients."

"And start meddling in their love lives," Lindsey interjected, rubbing her palms together.

The party had them both keyed up, and the anticipation was finally overshadowing Jenna's trepidation regarding her own love life. At least temporarily.

Tina took a seat in the guest chair. Her wedding ring was formidable, big enough to make up for the fact that the other two thirds of the party organizers were commitment experts in theory only.

"So, tell me more about how everything's been for you two so far."

Lindsey made coffee while they chatted, Tina assuring them that all their concerns were totally normal, and giving them great advice for how to approach the partygoers.

Finally Jenna glanced at the clock, surprised to find it was nearly three. "We better head out. The staff are expecting us in a half hour. Did you want to come, Tina, or do you need to get settled in your hotel...?"

"Lucky for me, that *is* my hotel. And I drove up, so if you can tell me where to go, I'll take us over."

"Perfect, thank you."

Just as Jenna was locking the office behind them, loud snatches of a debate rose from the gym stairs.

Nobody bleeding, nobody bleeding.

She recognized Mercer's voice a moment later, then he and Rich came into view, dressed in street clothes, looking fairly nonthreatening, except perhaps for Mercer's scrambled nose and the prominent white bandage on Rich's temple. They were deep in conversation, the volume clearly evidence of enthusiasm, not anger.

"Definitely some potential," Mercer was saying.

Rich let loose a long, low whistle. "That kid with the glasses?"

Mercer nodded. "Justin. Yeah."

"What?" Jenna asked as they approached the women.

"We had a kids' clinic this afternoon," he explained. "Just got out."

"He could be good," Rich said to Mercer.

"I know. Damn good." He turned back to Jenna with a quick wave to Lindsey and Tina. "Everything all set for the party?"

"Yes, thanks. Guys, this is Tina Maxwell. The franchise standards overseer. Tina, this is Mercer Rowley—"

They shook.

"And Rich Estrada."

"Pleasure," Rich said smoothly.

"Mercer and Rich run my late father's gym," Jenna said, making a snap decision to not mention that she and Mercer were involved. Things were complicated enough as it was.

Tina's smile tightened.

"They know," Jenna added softly. "That it's closing."

"I see. Well, nice to meet you, gentlemen."

Jenna felt she really ought to mention that these were also the guys who'd be filling in as security that evening, but judging from Tina's expression, she decided it might be best to spring that on her later, once it was too late for plans to be changed.

"Well," Jenna said awkwardly. "We better head over."

"See you later," Mercer said.

Jenna ushered the women toward the exit before Tina had a chance to learn just how soon "later" actually was.

13

MERCER WASN'T SURE about this plan.

He shuttled hangers around, debating what to wear. Maybe he ought to just back out on his agreement to play bouncer. Rich's idea, so no surprise it was a reckless one.

But he'd said yes. And he wanted to help Jenna. And fine, he was dying of curiosity about what a matchmaking mixer might look like and, more to the point, what sorts of eligible men she'd be so intimately—if professionally—involved with day in and day out at her new job. But as much as he wanted to know, he also thought maybe it was best if he didn't. Just like he'd never make Jenna come to a fight with him, knowing she'd cringe and gasp her way through it. He'd have to be nice to that Tina woman all night, acting as though she wasn't the one who'd brought the ax down on the gym.

But no point fighting it—if Jenna needed him, he'd be there. Loyalty knew no logic or pride, and what he felt for Jenna went far beyond loyalty. It had to be love. Nothing made a man this stupid except love. Hell, just ask Monty Wilinski.

He selected a plain black collared shirt and his gray all-purpose wedding-slash-funeral-slash-rare-press-appearance slacks, praying he remembered how to use an iron. Or where he'd last left his ironing board.

This scary, raw hurt in his heart and craziness in his head were the reasons he'd never been in a rush to get serious with anyone. Care about somebody enough and suddenly you quit acting logically. It was probably a good thing that their romance had an expiration date. It'd hurt to say goodbye to her, but at least life would go back to feeling simple, and he'd once again know the lay of his priorities.

He found the ironing board in the pantry and managed to press his shirt and pants without burning them. He dressed, feeling funny in these clothes. As requested, he'd gone casual for Monty's ash-scattering at the waterfront, then everyone had spent the evening eating roast beef sandwiches and drinking too much vodka in the gym, watching the hours-long DVD Monty and Mercer had put together of his all-time favorite fights. That had been a party. A party with a lot of sloppy, drunken, manly crying in the wee hours, but a celebration nonetheless. He felt more dressed for a wake now, a kickoff of the slow dismantling of Wilinski's Fight Academy...

Jesus, when had he gotten so mopey? He ordered himself to quit thinking so hard about everything. Like that ever did anybody any good. He must have caught it from Jenna.

He heard the door open and called, "I'm in my room."

"Cool. I have to get dressed," she called back.

After ten minutes she appeared in his doorway, just as he was lacing the dress shoes he'd unearthed at the bottom of his closet.

"Oh," she said. "Well, you look very handsome."

He stood to check that he'd gotten all the buttons, then tucked his shirt into his pants. He stretched his arms, the fit feeling a bit tight in the shoulders. "Jeez, I've let myself go since I last wore this. I must have bought it when I was in training."

She laughed. "Oh yes, you're a real tub, Mr. Zero Percent Body Fat."

a look in the full-

aiter if you wear one.

s he checked the results
ow about you? How you

bout that kind of
ving to figure out
o make her head
zes we're work-

I dunno."
ve it another

k. "You'll be periphery, and finally turned

ect. Her dress was short, but not
th his. This exy, deep red with a tan pattern,
ng enough ng.
the apart- e professional version of 'hot'?"
the entire g down at her dress. "I was going for

ort ride cked hot. You're going to steal all your
a stick, ts."

ot. But thank you. You look awfully hot
mem-
when nent on my usual style, I'm sure."
She s... "I quite like you dressed to fight, with your
arms showing.... But it's definitely best you keep covered up.
Those muscles may keep any tipsy people from getting rowdy,
but they'll also ruin my female clients' focus."

He shrugged the compliment away. "It's Rich you ought
o be worried about."

"Yes, we'll see how that goes. Maybe I'll just shove Lind-
y in front of him every few minutes as bait."

"I'll tell him if he's getting too…too like *Rich* with any-
," Mercer promised.

You weren't…? It didn't hurt your feelings that I didn't
duce you as my, you know, boyfriend to Tina earlier?"

He shook his head. "Only girls worry a[...] stuff. Plus she looked constipated enough tr[...] how to be polite to me and Rich. No need t[...] explode. Save that for tonight when she reali[...] ing security."

"Okay. As long as I didn't make you feel…[...]

He smiled. "I dunno, either. So don't g[...] thought. I'm ready if you want a ride over."

"If you're sure." She glanced at his alarm clo[...] stuck standing around a lot."

"Same as I'd be doing here."

She crooked her elbow and Mercer linked it wi[...] was how it might've felt if they'd been together lo[...] to attend a wedding as a couple. Mercer shut off[...] ment lights behind them, hand on her lower back[...] trip down the stairs and out to the car.

JENNA WISHED SHE could hold Mercer's hand on the sh[...] to the waterfront hotel, but sadly his old sedan was[...] and Boston driving involved constant shifting.

She stole glances at him in the streetlight, trying to re[...] ber a time when his face had been that of a stranger's, [...] his unusual features had intimidated her, instead of endearing her as they did now. Trying to remember a time when she'd pictured her dream guy as clean-cut handsome, with a nice car and an impressive income, a master's in something. How foolish she'd been, to think those things factored into manhood.

She was proud to cross through the upscale lobby with[...] him, arm in arm with the most wonderful man she'd ever me[...] And the last man whose heart she'd have chosen to break, ha[...] she gone into all this knowing what she did now about hi[...] about her father, about the gym her neighbors—and inde[...] Jenna—had been so quick to condemn.

Lindsey had brought her party clothes and makeup [...]

her, volunteering to get changed at the hotel so she could keep the decorating and organizing under control. By the time Jenna and Mercer arrived in the function room, all that was missing were guests and music. Jenna waved at Lindsey, who'd changed into a skirt and sweater and boots, the outfit keeping her more firmly on the professional side of the fence than Jenna's choice.

"Did I dress too much for a party?" she asked Mercer.

"It *is* a party."

"But I'm working."

He laughed. "You're also giving an introduction speech, during which I imagine you'll mention that you own the business."

"Yeah, true."

"So don't panic. You look like a woman who knows how to attend a cocktail party and get respectful attention from men."

"Right. Good."

Lindsey finished talking to the man behind the DJ's table and crossed the hardwood floor. "Hey, guys. You look great, Jenna. You too, Mercer."

"Hey yourself," Jenna said. "You've been busy since I ditched you to change."

"Yup. Oh and I found that clipboard and the name badges. They were hiding under a spare tablecloth."

Jenna sighed her relief. "Excellent. I'm going to be on door duty to start, so I can introduce myself as people arrive. Then I'll ask you to take over when Tina and I are doing the welcome spiel."

"No problem."

Lindsey led them around to ask Jenna's opinion on table placements, lighting, decorations. Mercer seemed to take everything in with detached interest, gaze darting with the scouting precision of a fighter—or, for this evening, a security guard.

"Looks great," he finally said.

"Really? To a guy, even?"

"Sure. Not too girlie, not too schmoozy. Not too stuffy, like an office party. It's nice. Kind of relaxing, with the lights all dimmed. Gives it that bar-feel, makes a guy feel like he's on the prowl. Or whatever the non-seedy word for prowling is."

Lindsey grinned. "That must be good, right?"

"What time is it now?" Jenna asked, digging for her phone. "Oh God, it's six." Only an hour until showtime.

"I better go down to the lobby," Mercer said. "I'm meeting Rich there to chat with somebody from the hotel's personnel about emergency procedures."

Jenna stood on her tiptoes to accept Mercer's kiss. "See you soon."

"Don't forget to breathe," he whispered, and headed for the door.

"When's Tina coming back?" Lindsey asked. "Oh—never mind."

Jenna turned in time to see Mercer holding the door for Tina, who'd gone to her room to change into a simple-but-chic gray skirt suit. If she recognized Mercer from their introduction that afternoon, she didn't show it. She crossed the floor and clasped her hands, beaming as if it were Jenna's wedding day.

"Ladies," she said warmly. "One hour till game time."

"If it makes sense to you," Jenna said, "I thought I'd do the greeting-people-and-handing-out-name-tags thing until maybe seven-thirty, give people time to trickle in, then we can do the welcome speeches?"

"Sounds perfect," Tina said. "Wonderful centerpieces, by the way. Great icebreakers."

"The cards were Lindsey's stroke of genius," Jenna said.

Lindsey dismissed the credit with a wave. "Oh—that's my bartender," she said, glancing across the room. "I mean, the guy I always hire when he's free, not my personal bartender. I'll get him set up and introduced to the waiters."

She disappeared, leaving Jenna and Tina to look around the space. Jenna wondered if this was how a bride felt, gazing around her reception hall, hoping her guests would have a good time.... Well, a bit different, since her romance wasn't at the center of the festivities. A sad thought dragged her down. This evening, and indeed this business, could mark the start of any number of people's love stories, but it was kicking off the demise of her own affair.

Tina patted her arm. "Don't worry. Just have fun."

"Yes, thank you. I'm sure I will."

Jenna puttered for a half hour, making sure everything was as it should be. She lit the candles on the tables and windowsills, annoyed the DJ by jogging to every corner of the room and double-checking the speaker volume. Mercer and Rich entered at twenty to seven. With the exception of the freshly stitched gash beside his eye, Rich looked as if he belonged at a *GQ* cover shoot in his black slacks and a dark, pressed shirt pinned with the promised security badge. A dark *purple* shirt, Jenna noted. Lindsey swept over, digging in her purse. Jenna approached as she began to dab foundation on Rich's cut.

"It'll help," Lindsey insisted.

He raised an eyebrow, wrecking her touch-up. "You're practically albino—it'll look ridiculous."

"It'll blend. It's better than a flesh wound. There." She snapped her compact closed.

"What's the flirtation policy?" Rich asked Jenna, with a whip-fast glance at Lindsey.

"Flirting is fine," Jenna said. "It's a flirty event. Feel free to make my female clients feel charming and attractive. Just, you know…"

"Don't poach," Mercer said.

Jenna nodded. "Flirt and flatter, but do please steer them toward the actual attendees."

Rich nodded. "Will do."

"One of us will loiter by the door to start, while you're signing people in," Mercer said. "Then once the party's under way, Rich and I will probably just wander, looking for trouble, asking the bartender if anybody's been making themselves too familiar." He glanced around the room as Lindsey fussed with the dimmer. "Though I'll be shocked if you wind up needing us. If anything, you'll need chaperones. This whole room's like one big invitation to make out."

"Especially those booth things," Rich said, pointing to the three half-curtained alcoves along one wall, each with wraparound cushioned benches and candlelit tables.

"That's why I picked this room," Jenna said. "Thought they'd be perfect if people hit it off and wanted a quiet place to talk."

"And exchange numbers," Rich said. "Or fluids."

She rolled her eyes. "The curtains don't close all the way. And if a few people swap numbers without actually signing up for the service, they'll still associate Spark with this party. Leaving them with a great impression of the business and the other clients is the most important thing."

"Jenna, I think your first guests are here," Mercer said.

"What? Oh God." She looked to the door and he was right—three women had arrived, dressed to mingle, and were looking around the room. Jenna hurried over.

"Hello! Are you ladies here for the Spark mixer?"

They were, and Jenna found their names on her list and their tags. "You're our first arrivals, so feel free to grab a glass of something and enjoy the atmosphere. We're recommending a two-drink maximum, just so you're aware."

She ushered them into the room then dashed to the DJ's table to get the music going. And all at once, it was a party.

At least half the guests arrived on time, and Jenna and Tina manned the door, getting everyone's names checked off and tags handed out. Jenna panicked for the first ten minutes, as the women streaming through the door vastly outnumbered the men. But the guys began showing up soon enough. As predicted, they were lousy at following RSVP directions and several had brought along buddies, so the gender balance was quickly evening out. Luckily, Jenna's list included the names of everyone she'd invited, not only those who'd confirmed.

A sharp-dressed man arrived solo, and she scanned the list for his name.

"I'm sorry, Todd, I'm not seeing you on here." She frowned her apology.

"I heard from a friend about the party."

"Oh, well, it's invitation-only." Not just to make Spark seem more exclusive, but to keep numbers manageable and discourage crashers. "Is your friend here? What's his or her name? As long as they'll vouch for you, that'll be fine—"

"I thought I'd surprise her, actually."

Something in his voice made Jenna uneasy, but Tina swept in.

"I'm sure it's fine to make an exception, just this once." Tina's tone made it plain that a guy as good-looking and nicely dressed as this one was welcome to party-crash. "I think Lindsey packed some blank name tags."

"She did, yes. Sorry." Jenna found him a tag and wrote his name in silver to match the other guests. "Welcome, Todd. Enjoy the party."

More and more guests arrived, and soon the chatter and laughter was drowning out the music, just as Jenna had hoped it might. Lindsey interrupted at seven-thirty, taking over greeting duties so Jenna and Tina could do the welcome at a podium set up in front of the DJ's station.

Heart hammering, Jenna waited for the music to fade, then turned on the microphone.

"Welcome," she said, pleased when a few people replied with friendly good-evenings. "Thank you all so much for coming tonight to help us kick off the grand opening of the Boston branch of Spark, the Northeast's leading traditional matchmaking service."

She waited for the polite applause, smiling out at all the faces. Everyone looked as hopeful and eager as she felt.

"I'll keep it short and sweet. My name is Jenna Wilinski, and I'm the owner and head matchmaker for Spark: Boston. This is Tina Maxwell, one of the original founders of Spark and my benevolent boss, and the lovely young woman in the red sweater now standing by the door is another matchmaker, Lindsey Tuttle. If you have questions about the service, feel free to ask any of us. We can also help get you signed up, and if you choose to do so tonight, your first month's membership will be fifty percent off."

Murmurs of intrigue—music to Jenna's ears.

"But basically, we just want you to enjoy a drink or two on us, meet some great local singles and have fun. So, welcome!" She beamed out a final smile and handed the mic to Tina. Jenna didn't absorb much of what Tina said. She was high on adrenaline, thrilled by all the people who'd turned out, hoping to find romance tonight. Best job in the world.

Before long Tina's opening remarks were wrapped and the music started back up, the scariest bit of the evening suddenly over.

"You did wonderfully," Tina said as they made their way through the crowd, introducing themselves to guests and answering membership questions.

"I was afraid I'd start stammering, but that was fun. Like making a wedding toast."

Jenna smiled at Mercer as their paths crossed. He wrecked his stoic act to give her a smile and thumbs-up.

"Thanks," she mouthed.

"He looks so familiar to me," Tina said.

Jenna kept her lips zipped. It didn't bother her one bit if Tina didn't recognize Mercer all dressed up. They continued to circulate, then Tina went to relieve Lindsey of door duties so she could enjoy mingling as well.

After a half hour of pleasant chatting, a sound jerked Jenna's head to the side—the high, shallow pitch of fear.

"Oh my God, it's Todd," a petite woman said to her friend.

"Shit. How did he know you'd be here?"

"Facebook, probably."

"Oh, Rachel."

"Did he see me yet? God, I have to go."

"Excuse me," Jenna said, butting in. "Is something the matter?"

"It's my psycho ex," the woman named Rachel said, pointing to the well-dressed, uninvited man Tina had allowed in. He was chatting to a woman at a table near the entrance, but his gaze was unmistakably drawn in Rachel's direction every few seconds. "He must have seen online that I'd be here."

"Is he dangerous?" Jenna asked, an easy, cool calm dropping over her to quiet her nerves.

"Not *dangerous,*" Rachel said. "But he's pushy and controlling and he'll make a scene if he sees me talking to any— Oh God, I just made eye contact with him."

"Don't panic. I'll take care of it." Jenna managed to catch Mercer's gaze and drew him over.

He met her a few paces from Rachel and her friend. "What's going on?"

"There's a man here who's upsetting one of these women. Her ex-boyfriend. Of the apparently psycho variety. Would you stay with her, make her feel safe, offer to call her a cab and escort her out if she's afraid? She's the one in the polka-dot dress."

He looked over Jenna's shoulder and nodded. "Sure. What about the guy?"

"I'm on it. I'm going to smooth things over if I can, but Rich is by the door if the guy won't leave without a fight."

"Be careful."

She touched his shoulder. "I will. Thank you."

She crossed the floor, staring right at Todd, filled with assertiveness for her mission. Rich was nearby, and the change in his posture indicated he knew something was amiss. He gave her a look and she shot one back, telling him to stay on the alert.

"Excuse me," she said to the woman Todd was talking to. "I'm Jenna, the owner of Spark: Boston?" There were cursory introductions then Jenna said, "Would you forgive me if I stole Todd away from you for just a moment?"

The woman politely wandered off and Jenna dropped her charming act.

"There's a woman here who's very upset that you've come."

Todd sighed, utter petulance. "She's such a drama queen. We dated, we broke up, and she just can't get over that."

"She's not the one who conned her way into her ex's plans, so I'm not entirely believing your side of things," Jenna said. "But your being here is making her uncomfortable, so I'm going to ask you to leave."

"This is a public event," he said, and his breath suggested he hadn't adhered to the drink maximum.

"No, this is a private event," Jenna said. "Invitation-only. And she was invited, not you."

"Well, she invited me, then," he said, pointing at Tina across the room.

"And I own this business and I'm uninviting you. You're upsetting my guest and I'm politely asking you to leave."

"And I'm politely declining."

"Then I'm going to have you politely removed by security." She jerked her head and Rich walked over.

"Problem?"

"I was invited," the guy said. He tapped his drink to his name badge, splashing himself with his martini. "You can't make me leave."

"Bet you I can," Rich said, crossing his arms.

"Professional, please," Jenna whispered.

"I *assure* you I can," Rich corrected in a studious tone.

"Go ahead and try, Rent-a-Cop."

Rich blinked and Jenna cringed. Bad enough he was here as a favor to her. Now he was getting insulted by a drunk and not even getting paid for it.

"I'm a black belt," the drunk guy went on.

Rich grinned. "Are you, then?"

Jenna felt panic setting in. She needed the levelheaded mercenary, not the hot-blooded one. "Rich, switch places with Mercer."

He gave her a look, his parade clearly rained on.

"Now."

He shot the guy a sneer and left to fetch Mercer.

"So," Jenna said, stalling. "You know one of my other guests?"

"Oh yeah, I know that bitch. And trust me, you don't want her in your little dating club. She's a *heartless slut!*" He shouted the final two words and Jenna felt spittle fleck her face. Her blood came to a boil. Nobody wrecked her party and upset her guests.

"Okay. That's enough. Get out right now, or I'll call the police."

Mercer arrived, face stony.

"This man needs to be escorted off the premises," Jenna

told him. "And if he gives you any trouble on the way down, have hotel security detain him and call the police."

"What?" Todd said, feigning outrageous indignation.

"You heard her," Mercer said, taking the guy by the upper arm.

He thrashed out Mercer's grip, his drink splashing across Jenna's dress. *Charming.*

"Rachel," he yelled. "Rachel!"

He seemed poised to make a run for his ex, but Mercer grabbed his wrist and twisted his arm up behind his back.

"Ow, Jesus!"

Jenna watched with a mix of anger and pride as Mercer angled his arm more sharply, doubling the guy over and shuffling him toward the elevators.

Once they disappeared, she strode across the floor, smiling calmly and scouting for any upset guests. No one looked too perturbed. Hopefully people assumed it was a case of one-cocktail-too-many. She worried Rachel and her friend had left, destined to cross paths with Todd in the lobby, but she eventually found them in one of the private alcoves. Rich was sitting next to Rachel, Tina hovering nearby.

"He's gone," Jenna said.

Rachel looked rattled, but not traumatized. "Good. Thank you." She sighed and shook her head. "That'll teach me to blab on Facebook."

"Have you got a restraining order against that guy?" Rich asked.

"No. He's never hurt me. He just gets drunk and calls me, all upset and demanding I explain why I dumped him. Once he showed up at my work. He always just wants to talk."

"Get a restraining order," Rich said. "Before he wants to do more than talk."

Jenna felt tired and thoroughly sober, slapped by proof of this darker side of dating.

"I'm so sorry," she said. "I take full responsibility for what happened, and I promise you it will never happen again."

Tina cut in. "Nonsense. I'm the one who should apologize," she said to Rachel. "I let him in without an invitation, after Jenna turned him away. This has *never* happened before at any of the dozens of Spark events I've overseen. I'm going to give you my direct number, if you need to talk about any of this."

Translation, Jenna thought, *please don't sue us.* Thank goodness Tina knew the drill, though. This job was going to prove far more interesting than she'd imagined.

They spent a few minutes making sure Rachel was calm, assuring her Todd wouldn't be returning. Rich even managed to get a laugh out of her. She and her friend decided to stay for the rest of the party. Rachel was of the opinion that her ex had screwed with her head enough; she wasn't going to keep letting him ruin things for her. The two women thanked Jenna and Rich, and Tina led them off in search of wine and distraction, doing her damnedest to repair the damage from her earlier mistake.

"How is she?"

Jenna jumped, finding Mercer at her side. "Oh, hello. What happened with the psycho?"

"He got real mad and sloppy while I was talking to the security guys outside, so I got him hauled off to the drunk tank. A night locked up with Boston's less-well-dressed lushes ought to put his choices in perspective."

She smiled grimly. "Good to know Rachel won't have to worry that he might be outside someplace when she leaves."

"Nope. He's headed downtown as we speak."

"I'll be sure to offer her a cab voucher, if she needs one. And free membership for a month, if I haven't totally wrecked her opinion of the company." Jenna released a deep breath, feeling about eighty years old.

Mercer rubbed her back. "Don't sweat it. You've had your

first crisis, and you handled it just fine. Had to get it out of the way sometime, right?"

She turned to look up at him. That face, always so calm. "Thank you, Mercer."

"Just doing my job."

"Yeah. A job you're not even being paid for."

He shrugged. "You offered. Don't feel bad. Or if you do, blame your dad. It's his fault I can't help but be on your side."

"I've spent way too much of my life blaming my dad for stuff," she said quietly.

"Fine. Blame yourself, then. I did it for you, anyhow," he added, smirking at her. "Fondness, not duty."

She smiled at that. "Sure I can't pay you?"

"I accept alternative forms of gratitude," he said cockily.

"That's a very fine Rich impression."

He leaned in to kiss her and she accepted it gladly, wishing they were alone so she could thank him more thoroughly. She was about to inform him of such things, but the moment was interrupted as Tina walked over, seeming pale and frazzled, not a look she typically wore.

"Everything okay with that Rachel girl?" Mercer asked.

Tina nodded. "Yes, thanks to you and your colleague. Thank you, Mr....?"

"Rowley."

"Mr. Rowley." She paused, blinking, then went on. "The security company we've been using has apparently disbanded. I'd be very interested in discussing a possible contract...."

Jenna bit her lip. *Awkward.*

Mercer grinned. "You don't recognize me, do you?"

Tina blinked. "I... No, I guess I don't. Though you do look familiar."

"We met this afternoon, outside Jenna's office? Me and Rich?" He nodded across the floor at him. "We run the boxing gym?"

Tina gave a small, embarrassed laugh. "Oh God, of course you are. I'm so sorry, I didn't recognize you all...formal."

"We're just moonlighting, as a favor to Jenna."

"I see. Are you trained in security?"

"We're probably overtrained. We spend a lot of time prying large, angry men off each other, but sorry. Not looking to make it a career."

"Right." Tina seemed to be coming to grips with the fact that she'd earlier written Mercer and Rich off as large, angry men. "Well, thank you very much for offering to help. You've really come through. And forgive me for not recognizing you. I feel so stupid."

Mercer shrugged, hiding the annoyance he must be feeling.

Tina had likely seen them kissing, so Jenna went ahead and took Mercer's hand. "Mercer and Rich volunteered to come tonight, to help me out." A thought occurred to her, and she felt some gear kick in, some latent gene she must have inherited from her father spotting a weakness, springing to life and lunging forward to take advantage of it.

"If you really are impressed and grateful," she said smoothly, "I'm sure Mercer and Rich would appreciate a chance to have a meeting with you, and plead their case about you reconsidering the fate of the gym?"

Tina's eyebrows rose.

"I'd appreciate it, too. I know you told me before it was a done deal, but maybe in light of everything that's happened tonight..."

"Um, yes. A meeting can't hurt."

"Looks can be deceiving," Jenna went on, milking her advantage. "The gym's not as seedy as everyone says. Not even close. The place could just use a little polishing, maybe a face-lift. A new sign, maybe redo the entryway, new hardwood stairs and railing. All improvements Mercer had hoped to make anyway. And far less invasive than the construction a new business in that space might demand—"

Mercer nudged her. "I think she gets the picture."

Tina smiled tightly and nodded. "You're right, it's worth a talk. I've certainly had my mind changed tonight. And I'll happily go to bat for you with the board."

Jenna supplied the rest. *I'll happily go to bat for you...if you're kind enough to not mention how I violated procedure and personally invited a stalker to your mixer.* Not blackmail, she assured herself. Just a bit of leverage. Jenna had to smirk at that, the idea that she might just have a bit of the shady businesswoman in her. She was more her father's daughter than she'd realized.

Once Tina turned away to continue circulating, Jenna squeezed Mercer's hand.

"You allowed to have a drink, after all that excitement?" he asked.

She looked around. Everyone seemed to be socializing just fine without assistance. "I guess I could spare five minutes to catch my breath."

Mercer led her to an empty alcove then fetched her a small glass of wine. He sat sideways in the booth, dutifully facing the party, but it felt nice to be alone with him, just for a few moments.

"Thank you, again," she said.

"Thank *you*." He shot her a gigantic grin. "You don't actually think we stand a chance, do you? Her letting the gym stay open?"

"Jesus, I hope so. If I can keep managing to channel my dad's business sense, yeah, I think it may be possible. Plus it's Tina's decision. There's no so-called board to take it to— she's the final word when it comes to that stuff. She'll just take a bit of finessing."

Jenna sighed, her adrenaline draining like bathwater. The

reversal had happened so quickly. The possibility that the gym could stay was all at once real and glorious. That Mercer could stay, in her city, her life, her bed… She'd fight for that. Tooth and nail, kicking and screaming.

"It doesn't solve everything, though," Mercer said. "Having the permission won't fix a thing if I can't manage to get the gym profitable again."

"No, but I have faith in you. And I'll help in whatever way I can."

"Like screaming your lungs out when Rich and Delante clean up at the tournament in two weeks?"

"As long as I can do that without actually having my eyes open for the carnage, then yes, absolutely." She sighed, gazing around the party for a minute, collecting her thoughts. "Will you keep living in the apartment if the gym stays put?"

"If you'll have me."

"Now that's a silly question. The real question is, which bedroom do we consolidate ourselves in?"

He smiled and looked down at the table, suddenly cagey.

"What? Am I being too optimistic?" she asked.

"Nah, go ahead and be optimistic."

"What, then?"

His smile deepened to a smirk. "We've been living together for a month, and sleeping together almost as long."

She nodded.

"And we're making plans to *keep* living together. Just seems kinda out of order. I haven't even taken you out on a date yet."

She laughed, realizing it was true. "Well, we've both been busy."

"I can at least tell you I'm in love with you," he said.

Jenna blinked.

"Before we're officially shacking up in the same bedroom," he went on. "I can at least do *that* in the right order."

Jenna tried to smile to keep from crying, different parts

of her face fighting to be the one to express her happiness. "Wow," she said, voice unsteady.

"You surprised?" he asked.

"Well, not entirely. I mean, I'm in love with *you*. I'd hoped maybe you felt the same way. I just… I didn't think you'd be so easy to tease those words out of."

He shrugged. "I know when I'm beat. You win by submission."

She was grateful he was turning it into a little game. Now wasn't the time to get all overwhelmed by the messy euphoria of her own blossoming romance. Business came first tonight. "We'll talk more about this at home, Mr. Rowley." She drained her glass and Mercer preceded her from the booth, giving her a hand as she stepped down.

He scanned the crowd before checking his phone. "When's this thing over?"

"Ten. But I probably won't be free to go until eleven."

"Hour and a half, then."

"Until you can finally escape my idea of a good time and get out of those clothes," she teased.

"Nope. Hour and a half until we can beat it home so I can rip that dress off you."

Jenna blushed. "Well. I'll see if I can't speed up the dismantling, maybe get it down to an hour and fifteen."

He kissed her, quick and firm. "Yeah. You do that."

14

THEY GOT HOME LATE the evening of their first real date—
dinner followed by drinks, the latter venue crashed by half a
dozen of the guys from Wilinski's, turning their quiet night-
cap into an impromptu party.

Mercer tossed his car keys on the coffee table. "Remind
me never to let Rich in on my romantic plans. I may as well
invite the entire gym."

"Aw, it was fun. Made me feel like an official part of the
clan. Though I could have done without a couple of those
rounds." She set her bag down. "Especially since I'm dating
such a teetotaler."

"Hey, I did a tequila shot with Rich. And I'll be ending all
that torture soon enough," he said, meaning once the tournament wrapped come Friday.

Jenna couldn't wait for it to be over—so much was riding
on Rich's and Delante's fights. Their outcomes would have
very real effects on the financial future of Wilinski's, and
the suspense was killing her. But for now, she was relieved
merely to be home after a long night—home with her man.
She was still acclimating to the reality that he was staying,
that he was hers for keeps. It had taken an awful lot of ha-
ranguing phone calls for Tina to come through with the of-

ficial amendment to the Boston branch's paperwork. Jenna wouldn't have put herself above a bit of hair-pulling, had it somehow come down to that. Hanging around all these fighters was having some very odd—but undeniably useful—effects on her business bloodlust.

She sank onto the couch with a huff. "Three more days."

"Don't have to tell me—I've got a countdown clock in my head." He bent to unlace his shoes.

"I hope you've got me sitting in the nosebleed section."

"Instead of a section close enough to see all the bloody noses?"

"Exactly. Though I think Lindsey might be up for that. I keep catching her on YouTube, watching MMA clips during her lunch break." Specifically clips of Rich's old matches, but Jenna kept that to herself. She only got to meddle in the love lives of people who paid her for the service…sadly.

She yawned, already exhausted to know she had to be up in six hours to start another workday. So much for the post-first-date debauchery she'd envisioned, if Mercer was as wiped as she was. "You want the bathroom first, or shall I?"

"No, stay comfortable. I need to get your opinion on something."

"Sure. What?"

Mercer disappeared into his former bedroom—now a sort of catchall space, one day to be a properly decorated guest room. Curious, Jenna sat up straight on the couch.

After a minute, the spare-room light went out and Mercer reappeared with a booklet in his hand. One of those college prospectuses? Jenna perked up, eager to hear about his plans once the tournament was through and he got a break from orbiting around Delante's potential.

He opened the booklet to a dog-eared page, passing it to her. "Tell me what you think of this."

Jenna's breath caught. It was a slick, glossy pamphlet from

a jeweler, and Mercer leaned down to tap a photo of a ring that had been starred.

An *engagement* ring.

"It's gorgeous." A simple design, with one larger diamond in the middle, three tiny ones bracketing it on either side.

"Is it your style?"

"It's gorgeous," she repeated dumbly.

"It's also insanely expensive."

"I'm sure. But we've been dating officially for, like, a minute. I love you, trust me, but why are you showing me this?"

He laughed and took the pamphlet back, studying it a moment. "Because next spring I'm gonna compete in a pro tournament for the first time in three years, and when I win, I'm buying it. And proposing to you." He met her gaze. "Then your hypercautious, by-the-book matchmaker brain will probably decide it's too soon, so I'll ask again the next month, then the next, and maybe a year from now, I'll get you to say yes."

"Oh" was all she could muster at first. "That's...that's very..."

His brow rose. "Deluded? Presumptuous? Romantic?"

"Well, it's you. It's very you. And it's a beautiful ring. I love it."

"You gonna tell me not to do all that stuff I just said?"

She let the giddiness fill her from the floor up. "I'm nervous to watch you fight. But no, I won't stop you from doing any of that."

His smile was slow and deep, mischievous. "You're an easier sell than I expected."

She blushed. "Well, it's a really beautiful ring."

Mercer laughed.

"You're right smart to think I might be cautious, given the time frame."

He skirted the table to sit beside her. "I went my whole life till I met you taking or leaving all this romance nonsense. I always knew if there was a woman out there who was right for me, I'd know it when I met her. And now I know it. So no point beating around the bush. It's you or bust. Plus your dad would murder me if I didn't make a decent woman of you, after all these weeks of sullying."

She poked him with her elbow. "And you seem pretty sure you'll win, huh?"

He nodded. "I will. I'll just remind myself that guy's standing between you and me and that ring on your finger, and it's a lock. What's your ring size?"

"I'm not sure."

"You got until March to find out."

She studied the photo again, boggled the diamond might be on her hand in less than six months. The "might" in that equation was all Mercer's, though—if he proposed, she'd accept, no question. She beamed a smile at him and he leaned in, held her face with his free hand and kissed her.

"I love you," she said as they separated.

"I love you. And I'm going to drive you absolutely bat-shit when I'm training, so just keep that picture handy so you know what you're suffering for. Eyes on the prize."

"Oh, right. Will I be cooking a lot of steaks come March?"

"That, and putting up with me spilling protein powder all over the counter, and swearing at the scale every morning, and quizzing you about everything that goes into whatever you make for dinner."

"For that ring, I'll gladly put up with all your psychoses, darling dearest."

He smiled, leaning back and seeming supremely happy and relaxed.

She gave his cheek a pat. "Don't you look smug?"

"It's that shot. I've got no alcohol tolerance anymore."

"Cheap date."

"You could totally take advantage of me right now if you wanted. I'm awful vulnerable."

She laughed. "No sex for three weeks before your future match, right? Wouldn't hurt to make up for that sadism, I suppose. And to keep perfecting all this sinful premarital nonsense, before you wreck it by proposing."

"Damn straight." He was on his feet, Jenna swept up in his arms in a breath.

She toyed with the zipper of his hoodie as he carried her to their bedroom and kicked her heels away. "Ding ding ding! Round one."

"Jesus Christ, how many rounds do you think I've got in me at two in the morning?"

"Fine. One will do, then. Just knock me out cold," she said as he carried her over the threshold.

He dumped her across the mattress and unzipped his jacket, a wicked smile brightening his dangerous features, strong body silhouetted by the light leaking in from the hall.

She sat on her heels, watching as he unbuttoned his shirt. "You're a very interesting man."

"That's a good thing, right?"

"Oh, that's a wicked good thing."

"Hey, there you go. Your dormant Boston accent's finally coming out." Mercer peeled off his socks and joined her on the mattress, kissing her deeply. Jenna urged him onto his back, hiking up her dress to straddle his waist. She smoothed her hands over his chest, musing.

"What?" he asked.

"Do you think this all really would've ended if the gym had to close? You really think you'd be moving to Philadelphia in a few months' time?"

"Yeah, I think I would."

She frowned. She'd secretly been hoping for a love-conquers-all reply.

"But I also think I would've found myself getting into my car at ungodly hours of the night, racking up speeding tickets and going broke buying gas to drive back up to Boston to see you."

"Oh." She remembered that night he'd driven from Hartford, right when she'd needed him. "That's a long drive."

"Six hours in a car would be nothing compared to lying alone in bed for, like, ten minutes, knowing I was in the wrong place."

She smiled at that and ran her palms down his exceptional arms. "You're quite the romantic."

"Nah, you just see romance everywhere, because of your job."

"Maybe. But I like what I'm looking at right now." She lowered onto her forearms to kiss him. "You're the Mr. Right I've been picturing all wrong my whole life," she mumbled against his lips.

"Good. Always happy to prove you wrong. What's my record now—like three and oh?"

She brushed her nose against his and smiled. "Shut up, darling."

"Think you can talk to me like that, because you're my boss and my landlady?"

"No, I can talk to you like that because I'm your future fiancée."

"Damn. I thought you were all traditional. What happened to love-honor-and-obey?"

"Like you really want that. Like you wouldn't prefer I put up a good fight."

He made a happy sound, a soft growl that hummed against her lips as he kissed her. She traced his nose and jaw with her fingertips, fascinated as ever by the man she'd fallen in love with. So much nicer to be proven wrong. So much nicer to enjoy life's surprises than for everything to go as planned.

And all so strange and unexpected, this new life she'd inherited. If she managed to make her clients feel even half as wonderful as she felt, she'd be acing her job.

"What?" Mercer asked after her fond preoccupation with his face had gone on for some time.

"Nothing. Just admiring you. Thinking about how awesome you are. That sort of thing."

"Oh, don't let me stop you. I mean, unless you could think all that stuff while we're having sex," he said, shifting beneath her and making his impatience plain.

"I'm sure I could try."

She laughed as he flipped them over, straddling her in the dim room, grinning down at her. She stroked his bare arms, anticipation lighting her up.

"Okay, then, Mr. Rowley. Show me what you've got."

* * * * *

COMING NEXT MONTH FROM

HARLEQUIN *Blaze*®

Available March 19, 2013

#743 THE RULE-BREAKER • *Uniformly Hot!*
by Rhonda Nelson

Army ranger Eli Weston is the proverbial good guy who desperately needs to be a little bad. But when temptation comes in the form of his fallen friend's former flame, he knows he's in trouble....

#744 NO ONE NEEDS TO KNOW
Made in Montana • by Debbi Rawlins

Annie Sheridan has a secret—she's on the run! Safe Haven animal shelter seemed like a good place to hide until she met Tucker Brennan, a man torn between bringing her to justice and taking her to bed.

#745 THE MIGHTY QUINNS: JACK
The Mighty Quinns • by Kate Hoffmann

Mia McMahon's wealthy widowed father has fallen in love with his old flame, Jack Quinn's mother. Unfortunately, neither Jack nor Mia is particularly happy about the romance. But luckily for their parents, they're too busy hitting the sheets to do much about it....

#746 CRASH LANDING • *Stop the Wedding!*
by Lori Wilde

Millionaire playboy Gibb Martin ends up stranded with tough-talking pilot Sophia Cruz on a deserted island. And it isn't long before Gibb and Sophia's high drama turns into fiery passion....

HBCNM0313

REQUEST YOUR FREE BOOKS!
2 FREE NOVELS PLUS 2 FREE GIFTS!

HARLEQUIN®

Blaze®

red-hot reads!

YES! Please send me 2 FREE Harlequin® Blaze™ novels and my 2 FREE gifts (gifts are worth about $10). After receiving them, if I don't wish to receive any more books, I can return the shipping statement marked "cancel." If I don't cancel, I will receive 4 brand-new novels every month and be billed just $4.49 per book in the U.S. or $4.96 per book in Canada. That's a savings of at least 14% off the cover price. It's quite a bargain. Shipping and handling is just 50¢ per book in the U.S. and 75¢ per book in Canada.* I understand that accepting the 2 free books and gifts places me under no obligation to buy anything. I can always return a shipment and cancel at any time. Even if I never buy another book, the two free books and gifts are mine to keep forever.

150/350 HDN FV42

Name _____ (PLEASE PRINT) _____

Address _____ Apt. # _____

City _____ State/Prov. _____ Zip/Postal Code _____

Signature (if under 18, a parent or guardian must sign) _____

Mail to the Harlequin® Reader Service:
IN U.S.A.: P.O. Box 1867, Buffalo, NY 14240-1867
IN CANADA: P.O. Box 609, Fort Erie, Ontario L2A 5X3

Want to try two free books from another line?
Call 1-800-873-8635 or visit www.ReaderService.com.

* Terms and prices subject to change without notice. Prices do not include applicable taxes. Sales tax applicable in N.Y. Canadian residents will be charged applicable taxes. Offer not valid in Quebec. This offer is limited to one order per household. Not valid for current subscribers to Harlequin Blaze books. All orders subject to credit approval. Credit or debit balances in a customer's account(s) may be offset by any other outstanding balance owed by or to the customer. Please allow 4 to 6 weeks for delivery. Offer available while quantities last.

Your Privacy—The Harlequin® Reader Service is committed to protecting your privacy. Our Privacy Policy is available online at www.ReaderService.com or upon request from the Harlequin Reader Service.

We make a portion of our mailing list available to reputable third parties that offer products we believe may interest you. If you prefer that we not exchange your name with third parties, or if you wish to clarify or modify your communication preferences, please visit us at www.ReaderService.com/consumerschoice or write to us at Harlequin Reader Service Preference Service, P.O. Box 9062, Buffalo, NY 14269. Include your complete name and address.

HB13R

It was her. He knew it.

Eli Weston chuckled low, the sound rife with irony, then brought the bottle to his lips once again. Southern Comfort—appropriate, considering that was the only form of relief he was likely to get during this godforsaken week from hell. Water sloshed against the side of the tub and splashed onto the back porch as he deliberately shifted into a more relaxed position. It didn't matter that he was wound tighter than a two-dollar watch, that the mere thought of her sent a bolt of heat directly into his groin.

Perception, naturally, was key.

How did he know it was her who'd pulled into the driveway? The particular sound of her car door? The crunch of a light-footed person across the gravel? Those keen senses honed by years of specialized military training?

Ha. As if.

Nothing that sophisticated, unfortunately. It was the tightening of his gut, the prickling of his skin across the nape of his neck, the slight hesitation from the moment the car motor turned off until the driver decided to exit the vehicle. As though

HBEXP79747

she was steeling herself, preparing to face him.

That was what had given her away.

"I'm back here," he called before she could mount the front porch steps.

She hesitated once again, then resumed movement and changed direction. Eli closed his eyes and prayed that she'd be in something other than that damned dress she'd had on earlier today. It was white, short and…flouncy. Not the least bit inappropriate, but somehow it managed to be sexy as hell all the same. It hugged her curvy frame, showcased her healthy tan and moved when she did. The hem fluttered just so with every swing of her hips, a silent "take me" with each step she took.

It was infuriatingly, unnervingly hot.

A startled "Oh" made him open his eyes, his gaze instinctively shifting toward the direction of the sound.

He mentally swore. Just his luck—she was still wearing it.

"There's a shower inside," she said tightly. "Could you get out of there? I need to talk to you."

He shrugged lazily, then stood. Water sloshed over the sides and sluiced down his body. He pushed his hair back from his face, careful to flex his biceps in the process.

He arched a deliberate brow. "Anything for you, sweetheart. Happy now?"

The last person Eli Weston can afford to be attracted to is the only woman he wants. Find out why by picking up THE RULE-BREAKER by Rhonda Nelson.

Available March 19.